Tread: Fallen Nation

Book 1

Jeff DeMarco

First Edition, 2019

Many thanks and my sincerest apologies to U.S. Military and government employees, of whom I've cast both protagonist's and antagonists within the novel. Quick disclaimer: This is a work of fiction. Names, characters, places, and incidents are the products of the author's imagination or are used fictitiously. Any resemblance to actual events, locales, or persons, living or dead, is entirely coincidental.

I've cast certain characters to be angry, violent, addicted, misguided, arrogant, abusive and downright treasonous. I don't personally know of any such polarizing characters in real life (thank goodness, my life is much less exciting). Furthermore, during my time in the military, I had the honor of serving with some of the finest individuals this country has ever known… but this novel isn't a memoir.

At the end of the day, my characters are all just human and for the sake of the story- their attributes, subversive organizations or actions were necessary to support a particular character arc. Furthermore, the novel is set in the near future as opposed to the present, so fingers crossed that none of this comes to pass.

To my wife, Nicole, whose continued support has made this all possible.

4 Tread: Fallen Nation

PROLOGUE

Centuries from slavery, we awoke as captives. In the first days of war, the American people were sorted, not based on the color of their skin or their religious beliefs; rather, based on whether they were a threat. Our daily burdens were of benefit to our true owners; we could not go or say or do as we wished; though we were not bound with chains, we were no longer *free*.

Decades before the first shots were fired, the process began. The great social engineers of mid-century, whether by ignorance or lack of understanding, did not foresee where their grand experiment would lead. By design, we sequestered ourselves with other like-minded individuals, caught in an echo chamber of our own opinions. We gave up on the ideal that *no man can own another,* and it happened so gradually that no one noticed. Those that did were either labeled as crazy or bigoted; those with proof were designated as a threat and eliminated, often committing suicide with two rounds to the back of the head.

Years ago, we were something to behold, and a target; the last beacon of light to be seen in the night sky, the last remaining stronghold of freedom on earth; each man and woman given a blank canvas to paint their own story. We could be that again, but not now, not yet. Hard times created strong people. Strong people, in turn created good times, in turn created weak people, in turn created hard times; and so, the pattern went, until the weak decided they no longer wanted hard times, for themselves.

They preyed on strength, not on a field of battle, nor in a fair fight, but an open forum of opinion. They cut the legs out from the strong, saying advantages in aptitude and assets were unfair, unjust, illegitimate. Ability was no longer a currency, but something to fear and suppress.

Those designers that orchestrated the end were made up of politicians and bureaucrats, church and crony business leaders on the governments dime, military and police leadership; their agents had worked themselves into key positions in every major organization within the US, influenced decisions through violence and extortion, slowly shaping the country into an unrecognizable shell of itself.

The people felt the strain, bending themselves further and harder as each year passed. Some wanted to fight, but wouldn't. Others did, without understanding the true nature and depth of their enemy; they died. All the designers needed now was a spark, something to justify the carnage that would ensue, and they would have what they always desired... absolute power.

Whether you wanted to know, whether you wanted to see the truth of the world we live in, it didn't matter anymore; everyone in every corner of this great country and every inch of the globe would come to realize – the fragile nature of our societies, our systems, our world, and the destructive, conquering force of human will. In the years of the second Civil War, and

before the great tribulation, hope failed in the darkest of
times.

8 Tread: Fallen Nation

CHAPTER 1

A single stinging bead of sweat dripped down into Staff Sergeant Evan Decker's eye. Without moving, he squeezed both eyes shut, as he didn't dare shudder or move, as he snipped the seventh of a chain of nine roadside bombs, set in a parallel circuit; a more complex setup than he'd seen in the last 15 months of his deployment. The latest batch of blasting caps were especially sensitive; intel had traced them back to a farming supply store in Iowa of all places. One false move and the C-4 filling the 155-howitzer round would ignite, and Evan would be just another poor bastard with his name etched on a plaque somewhere, his disassembled body parts stuffed into a sealed casket and laid to rest.

He thought about how the funeral team leader would take a knee in front of his mother and recite the words, "Ma'am, this flag is presented on behalf of a grateful nation, as a token of appreciation, for the honorable and faithful service rendered by your loved one," then render a salute. The funeral team would shoot their guns off, the bugler would play a recording of *Taps* from a speaker hidden inside the bell of his instrument. Everyone except his father would cry, and life would go on. To some extent, Evan was already resigned to this end. The threat would be eliminated, his buddies some 200 meters away would be safe, and no doubt they would have a replacement inside of a few days.

Nonetheless, he held his breath, as his vision blurred through the hot foggy face shield. The bomb disposal suit would catch most of the shrapnel, either in the chest plate or helmet, but would do little for the pressure wave. The blood vessels in his brain would rupture immediately, but not before an excruciating shot of pain across his body, as his limbs wrenched apart inside his Kevlar coffin.

The words, "Hurry up," sounded in his earpiece. "We got contact!"

'Snip,' the wire cutters sliced through IED 8 of 9. He heard movement up ahead, the tell-tale 'crack, crack, crack,' of an AK-47 in the distance. *Why hadn't they detonated the IED? Did he cut the main transmission wire, already?* He didn't know. A louder weapon sounded in the distance, a Russian-made DSKA machine gun maybe, bullets zipped above his head. Evan clawed at the ground to uncover *hopefully* the last explosive in the chain.

An insurgent yelled in Afghani Pashto up ahead, "Hurry forward!" Only a lone insurgent gunman sprinted ahead into the open – the bomb's triggerman.

A .50 caliber Heavy machine gun opened up behind him, hammering the rocky outcropping the enemy used as cover. The urge to pull his 9mil pistol nearly overtook him, as he fingered the pouch on his chest. "No," he whispered to himself, then flipped the knife open on his multi-tool and dug feverishly.

'Ping, ping,' bullets echoed off of the rock beside him, and his knife snagged something in the dirt. "What the hell?" he whispered, examining the three wires in series, connected by a small metal box. He'd never seen anything like it, not since EOD school, and even then, insurgents never took the time to make something so intricate. *And why just the one bomb? Why not all of them?* He took his knife blade and tried to bend up a flap on the metal casing, then saw the spring - booby trapped. His hands shifted down towards the howitzer round, a metal plate secured around the tip of the shell, in the void where the fuse would sit, securing the blasting cap from removal.

'Ping, ping,' two rounds impacted the dirt directly ahead of him, burying in the Kevlar armor covering his thigh, knocking him onto his side. Then he saw it, the side of the howitzer round, a bolt twisted into the metal, and also three separate ant trails of disturbed earth, concealing either detonating cord, transmission wire or both, branching off in different directions from the final explosive. Evan keyed his radio. "Cover fire!" He could feel his heartbeat in his leg now, as if someone hit him with a baseball bat.

"Artillery incoming!" sounded in his earpiece. "You're danger close, take cover!"

"Hold on!" He yelled back, flipping the Philips head screwdriver out from his multitool. He peeked up over the rock, looking for the triggerman. "I'm almost done. Keep that asshole away from the det-cord!"

"You got it!" A barrage of small arms fire opened up from behind; covering fire to keep enemy heads down.

Evan bore down on the screwdriver, finally breaking the bond of metal on metal. He lifted the cover slowly, peering inside the cavity. A small metal spring was visible and pressing against the metal cover, a copper transmission wire, covered in a blue plastic and soldered to the inside of the cover. *What the hell*, he thought. *This doesn't make sense. No bomb-maker would risk death to make a spring-loaded booby trap*, but enough with conjecture. "There it is," he whispered, careful to maintain metal on metal contact. He pulled a length of spare copper wire from his cargo pocket, wrapping one end around the spring, the other end around the wire soldered to the cover. That gave him room to fully remove the cover. He gripped the four sets of wires and pulled. Simultaneously a voice yelled in his earpiece, "Take cover!"

The last thing he remembered was the length of a silver blasting cap in his hand and out of the body of the howitzer round, then the blast - artillery fire 50 meters away, then pressure, then black. Moments before the blast, Evan felt anxious to go home, happy even. No, that's not right... happy isn't what Evan was, and *home* wasn't where he was going. Though, it would be the last bomb Evan would ever diffuse. From here on out, he would be the one to make them, plant them, detonate them.

◊

Where am I? Evan wondered, as shadows danced before his eyes. The world seemed cloudy and grey; murmurs sang through the ringing in his ears.

"They've called for a general retreat," a voice whispered. "He needs to be on the plane ASAP."

Evan recognized the voice as Captain Sayyid, his company commander.

Another voice rose. "He's got a significant traumatic brain injury, sir. Chances are he won't even wake up."

Sayyid grumbled. "I don't give a shit." Evan could sense his presence hovering over him. "Last ride home is wheels up in ten, Doc. I want him, and you on that plane, dead or alive."

"I've got seven others that I can't move," Doc said, a panic in his voice. "You need to hold that plane."

Evan's vision sharpened, focused on Sayyid's stern glare above him, and First Sergeant Baker a few steps away. "I'm not holding any- "

"I'm fine," Evan strained, reaching for the saline lock on his arm. A pain shot through the back of his skull straight through his eyes as he struggled to lift his head.

"Lay back," Doc whispered, as First Sergeant put both hands on Evan's shoulders.

Sayyid stared dead at Evan; he must not have realized Evan was listening. "Last days of war." He raised his arm and motioned for a team of Soldiers holding a litter. "We're going home."

"I gather." Evan rolled his eyes. His head was restrained in a collar, he peered over, up and down the tarmac – Bagram Airfield, a place he'd recognize any day. From Kandahar province it was a nine-hour drive, likely they would have flown him in a chinook. "Why the rush?"

"Don't worry about it," First Sergeant said, his voice tough as iron.

If they only knew, this was just the beginning.

Next thing Evan knew, he was rolled onto the litter and staring at the sky, his arms pinned at his sides against the litter. He dozed off for a moment, and woke on the floor, staring up at a white lit ceiling, camouflaged legs spread out at either side of him, the roar of a commercial airliner and pressurized cabin. *Odd,* he thought. *Everyone's got their weapons and armor still on.* "Hey, you!" he yelled, to anyone who would listen.

A young private turned his head. "Sergeant?" He had medium brown skin and tightly cropped hair, and a rasp, steely midwestern accent. "You're alive!" Through the fog, Evan Recognized him at once.

"Hayes, get me the hell out of here."

Another Soldier turned. "Leave him." It was Sergeant First Class Stokes, Evan's platoon sergeant. "Doc says he's not supposed to move."

"Fuck sake," Evan yelled. "I'm fine!"

Stokes crossed his arms, turned and huffed in his seat.

"I suppose you're gonna clean me up when I piss myself?" Evan asked, a serious edge to his voice.

Stokes turned, his normal angry stare, mixed with genuine concern.

"See?" Evan wiggled his feet and hands. "I'm fine."

Stokes nodded to Hayes, who bent down to loosen the straps.

"Here," Evan said, grasping Hayes' hand and pulling upward. Some of the pain subsided, perhaps the drugs they had given him. *Must have been morphine,* he knew the feeling, and the dizziness that persisted. "Feels like I got hit by a bus."

"I told your ass to take cover," Stokes grumbled. He was a stout black man, thinning hair trimmed short, and a thick, tight moustache along his lip gave him the look of someone much older than his 38 years. Stokes was a hammer, and as Evan's platoon sergeant, that occasionally made Evan the nail.

Evan rolled his eyes. "What happened? Why are we going back home?"

"Presidential order," Stokes said, pointing at the back of the plane, towards the lavatory sign. "Beyond that, I don't know."

"Got my assault pack?" Evan asked.

Stokes' eyes narrowed, as he hadn't taken any of the contents, but he knew exactly what was inside. "Quite a spread you've got there." He stood and lifted the overhead compartment, shook the bag around, making the many pill bottles rattle.

"Just taking my vitamins..." Evan laughed it off, as he had so many times before. His last bomb wasn't his first brush with death. The pills weren't helping, not the ones for anxiety anyhow. Evan was given the post-traumatic stress cocktail – reuptake inhibitors made to dull the edge, *crazy pills* he called them, just made him sleepy; he didn't take them. They gave him benzo's too, or benzodiazepine - *happy pills*, a mild euphoria that lasted no more than four hours, good for acute panic attacks and taking the edge off after an operation, though that wasn't his drug of choice. He wasn't so bad that he would dive for cover at a car backfire; the opposite in fact – he'd stand toe to toe with any threat, real or perceived. He found it hard to respond with anything but humor or rage.

He'd grown up an impetuous young man, often in trouble with one authority figure or another. In some ways, his military career focused him, trained him when to keep his mouth shut. Other ways, he'd risk far too much, far too often. He'd seen so much already, yet he still felt fear, though was gripped by it in a very

different way. He didn't have a death wish; he didn't
think so, anyhow. His hand ran compulsively across his
arm, a long red scar finally formed, stitches gone,
healed to the point of not needing bandages; his
memory evoked the large shard of metal that had once
been sticking out of his arm, a gift from his first month
in country. Despite that, he didn't take his ticket back to
the states. They gave him pain killers to go along with
his new purple heart – a chunk of polished metal and
ribbon he left somewhere, cast aside in the desert sands.
The physical pain had since waned, yet he lied; more
pain killers, he needed to feel numb; not just for his
own peace of mind, but to do his job, to save his
buddies. Now with the pain shooting into the base of
his head, and fresh, invisible scars, he needed them
more than ever. Standing at the tiny bathroom mirror,
he looked paler than normal. He took double the normal
dose of painkillers, despite his veins coursing with
morphine. With it came an immediate high, not from
the drug itself, rather like an addict getting his fix. *Soon*
he would feel 'normal.' *Am I an addict*? he wondered.
He didn't know.

Looking down at each face along the many
rows, he thought about his hometown briefly, walking
back to his stretcher. Evan was a cowboy, in a way. It
wasn't his intention, rather that's just the way he always
was. He would have been perfectly at home in a
cowboy hat and shit-kickers, but he didn't own either of
them. The way he stood, the way he spoke – not in a
southern drawl, as he was born and raised in northern
Wyoming, which was no longer a home to him. Rather

an odd combination of grit and ease, as though he could fall off his horse in the middle of nowhere and still walk back to town with a smile on his tanned face. The smile was gone now, the experiences of his last deployment were beyond his grasp.

It occurred that he didn't understand what was being said as he walked back to his stretcher. Not that he couldn't hear anything; nothing registered but a haze of noises.

Hours later, Doc stepped over Evan and knelt down. "How you feeling?" He shone a flashlight into Evan's eyes. Doc was a buck sergeant, technically by the last name of Santos, but as Soldiers do, everyone just called him Doc.

"Fine-ish," Evan said, somewhat annoyed at the intrusion.

"You've got some swelling, maybe even a bleed in there, I'd bet," Doc said, feeling around on the back of Evan's skull. "Any pressure?"

"Some."

"Lay still," Doc said, pressing Evan back down on the stretcher. "We don't have a surgeon onboard, and I'd hate to perform emergency cranial surgery on a hematoma."

Evan stared at him, cockeyed.

"You think I'm joking?" Doc said. "I've been running around here looking for a drill bit just in case I need to open your skull up."

"Hmm." Evan nodded. "Copy that, Doc."

Doc knelt down. "That was a really close one, Sergeant. I'm afraid that happens again, even if it's not as bad, you'll be going home in a body bag."

"I mean, you could make me wear a helmet." Evan grinned.

"I'm serious." Doc glare at him. "Any more head trauma, and you're toast."

Evan chuckled. "But how would I lick the windows?"

"Death, blindness, loss of motor function," Doc rattled off all the possible outcomes. "Nausea, seizures, mood swings, erectile dysfunct-"

"Whoa, Doc." Evan smirked. "Don't get blowed up again. I got it."

"Not just explosives. Impact too. I don't recommend any combatives training for a long while."

"Ok, ok." Evan rolled his eyes. "I got it."

"Good." Doc rose, and walked down the aisle toward his next patient. From what Evan could see, the next guy over had fared much worse than he; wrapped up like a mummy, blood soaking through bandages. At once, he felt lucky for at least having all his appendages intact.

He lay back on the stretcher, as all the seats were taken, popped his earphones in and tried to block out what he could of the world.

20 Tread: Fallen Nation

CHAPTER 2

Protesters had been drowned out by the sea of applause waiting at the gate. That was the last time he came back to the states. He recalled a crusty old Vietnam vet had nearly come to blows with a long-haired hipster, sporting a man-bun. Evan laughed at the sheer stupidity of it all. He joined for a lot of reasons – adventure, experience, the opportunity to blow shit up… But there was also a morality to it; so that others may live freely, to say and do as they wish, to include protesting Evan's existence, and in the case of the Vietnam vet, to put a figurative boot up hippy-ass. He was better back then, idealistic, not hurting the way he was now, and at least the protesters didn't spit, like his father told him they would. He heard no such fanfare today.

The Atlanta sunset shone brilliantly across the tarmac, with hues of crimson and violet; an earthly sea of burnt orange rolled in waves across the land as the sun dipped down below the horizon. His eyes deceived him, and for a moment it seemed that the whole of the world would be swallowed up in that beautiful sunset. 'Just landed, call in a bit.' Evan clicked send, while staring out through small windows at the magnificent sight, so fixated that he ran head-on into the herd of other Soldiers, now bottlenecked along the jetway to concourse F. He was numb now; as he'd just chewed up another oxycontin before landing; anything to keep from snapping at the welcoming party of veterans and patriots, likely a handful of protesters. They'd throw insults like "baby killer," and "murderer." At least, that's what Evan had experienced at his last return home from the sandbox.

Being called a "baby killer" stung. The fact of the matter was that he had killed children – carrying AK-47's and strapped with suicide vests. Forget everything you knew to be right or wrong; an insurgent remotely detonating a suicide vest on an innocent child, their tiny appendages blasting out many meters away was beyond cruel, it was beyond insidious. It was unthinkable. There were no words. He didn't know how he truly felt about a higher power, yet he prayed to God for the eternal suffering of those responsible.

Fallujah, Iraq, was his first deployment. He didn't know much Arabic, but enough to recognize the word, "Bomb." A little girl, no more than seven had come in to their dusty combat outpost. She was a regular, as everyone knew that cherubim smile, her tiny hands carrying a large wooden box filled with glasses of ice-cold coke. She would sell them to the Soldiers for fifty cents a cup, and no doubt use the money to feed her family.

One day she had no smile, her face was sheet white, hands gripping the sides of her box tighter than usual. Soldiers approached as normal, and for once she drew back. Evan watched from under a camo net, a respite from the midday sun. It didn't dawn on him until she started to babble frantically, as one by one, Soldier's took cup after cup from the box, tossing quarters into the box, and then he heard it... "Bomb!" her gentle voice, spoken in Arabic, as one final Soldier took his cold drink, and 'Boom!' He tried not to think what would have happened if he'd been up close and seen her odd mannerisms. Maybe he'd be dead. Maybe the little girl and all of his friends would still be alive.

The child soldiers toting AK's were another story, no less tragic. Their enemy would use a primitively concocted narcotic; slashing the buds of the opium poppy, gather up the fluids on a piece of gauze then boil It down into an injectable form. They used this to make the children fearless, feel no pain, kill without thought; once addicted they used it to control. *Odd*, Evan thought, drawing the parallel with his newfound habit. It was effective. Suppressive fire and non-kill shots had little effect. Center of the chest or the head, almost like they were zombies; frequently he would think, *Dear God, what have I become?* as he pictured standing over a child's tiny body. He held the child's hand in his memory, so much smaller than his own. *What have I done?*

Evan was OPCON to an infantry platoon, meaning that if there were no bombs to diffuse, he was a grunt. He put down many an insurgent, and after the first few it became easier. He seldom spoke of it. His mannerisms had grown cold in the preceding days, as those that look dead on the outside are often hiding an internal weakness. Despite the painkillers, he felt everything and in that he felt like a monster; war wasn't fun for him, killing wasn't glamorous, but an ugly thing that needed to be done for self-preservation; at least that's what they told him, and what he told himself to keep from… to keep himself alive. After each firefight, he wanted to die, part extreme exhaustion, part self-loathing that would creep up on him like a lead coat draped over his shoulders; each life he ended drug him further down into the pit he had spent a lifetime digging.

Ahead in the airport Evan heard murmurs up towards the exit into the concourse, an unease about them; a flicker of white outside caught his eye. Past the check-in desk, the terminal was silent but for the incessant click of combat boots marching along tile floors; no television nor conversation, no bustling passengers, no announcements across the loudspeakers. Only a sign that read, "SERVICE MEMBERS, DROP ALL WEAPONS AND EQUIPMENT HERE," with an arrow pointed to wheeled metal tables along the concourse. There were no lights burning in the darkened space, only sunlight shone through the western window, high atop the two-story hallway. As the camouflaged column of Soldiers neared the end of the concourse, he realized now what the flicker of white was.

Evan didn't remember the Captain's name, rather recognized her face as she stepped out of the pack, towards a security agent, garbed in a white hazmat suit and protective mask, rifle slung at the ready. He could hear the agent's shouts muffled through their mask. "Get back in line, Ma'am!" as the rifle raised.

The Captain put her hands up, as if to say *I'm not a threat*. "Tell me what's going on here?"

Evan slowed as he neared her position, shuffled through ceaseless flood of Soldiers and stood beside her. He recalled his hands only days ago, as they lay on the hard olive drab outer shell of the artillery round, clipping the wires that connected to the blasting cap. Death seemed so far away from them now, left along the mountain passes of Kandahar province, yet here it was staring them in the face.

He hoped perhaps his standing there beside her could somehow diffuse the situation, as he had the IED. Barely a breath issued from his mouth, he stood as still, as unthreatening as possible, though consciously his confusion and unease had turned to anger at the threat. His painkillers were in full effect, chemically induced restraint perhaps his only saving grace. He remembered her now; Captain Arden was an attractive, yet physically unremarkable woman, with short auburn hair and a round freckled face. He heard her speak once at a brigade level briefing, on her area of expertise in communications, then spoken to her briefly on a handful of occasions in passing. She had a kind and motherly demeanor, and more importantly, she knew her stuff.

Evan's muscles tensed as the agent's posture shifted – then swung the barrel from Captain Arden to him. Poised in his mind, he envisioned his left hand clutching the upper receiver, dragging the barrel down to the floor; His right hand balled into a fist, striking the agent in the temple of his chemical mask. Before he could make his move, he felt a gentle hand grab his wrist.

"You're going through decontamination!" the agent yelled. "You'll be briefed at your destination." He flipped the rifle's safety off. "Now, get back in line."

Evan heard it then, the tremble in the agent's voice – fear. *Of what?* he wondered, *what're they decontaminating us for?* He felt two sets of hands grab on to him, one pushing from the side, the other a rough set of hands wrapped underneath his arm and around his wrist. He looked back, Captain Arden pushing him forward, a sort of strength, yet persistent kindness in her green eyes, as if to say, *you're ok, now let's get the hell out of here.*

On the other side was Sergeant First Class Stokes, who had snatched him from inside the pack. "What the hell you thinkin'?" he growled. "Trying to get yourself shot?"

"What is this?" Evan whispered.

"Don't know," Stokes mumbled, peering over top the line of Soldiers ahead. "Keep your head down."

Up ahead and around a corner, a bullhorn sounded with instructions. The line of troops stopped dead, now milling in place, waiting their turn. As they rounded the corner, Evan could see the herd converging into a single file line, more armed security at the head of a white fabric tunnel, stretched towards the corners of the ceiling.

"Staff Sergeant Decker." The whisper came from behind him. "Does your cellphone work?"

"Yes, Ma'am." Evan reflexively reached into his pocket to check, a mild excitement that she remembered his name. He looked down, 'Message send failure.' "Scratch that, Ma'am. No signal… Think it means anything?"

He thought of the last in-flight announcement, the pilot's voice so smooth and confident that he hadn't thought anything of it. *"Ladies and Gentlemen, as we start our descent, please be advised we have no comms with the tower at this time, please make sure your seat backs and tray tables are in their full upright position. Make sure your seat belt is securely fastened and all carry-on luggage is stowed underneath the seat in front of you or in the overhead bins. Thank you." Was that what the pilot said?* Evan wondered. Now that he thought about, it seemed far more concerning, yet he reasoned it was the pilot's role to eliminate panic in the cabin.

"Probably," She whispered. "Remember when Russia invaded their neighbors down in Georgia? Hacked their communications network. If things go bad, be ready to run like hell."

"You remind me of someone," Evan whispered back.

"Remove all personal items from your pockets!" the controlling agent yelled through his bullhorn. "Once inside, you'll be instructed to remove your clothing. You'll move through a series of decontamination zones, prior to entry a blood sample will be collected and analyzed. Once inside, continue walking along the red line until ordered to stop. Once completed, you will be issued a new uniform, inoculated, and assigned to transportation towards your final destination…"

"Do me a favor, Ma'am." Evan looked back with a grin, as he wanted desperately to crack a joke, perhaps something about staring at his ass, but now was not the time.

"Mhm…" She rolled her eyes sheepishly, as though reading his mind.

"Cut that shit out, Decker," Sergeant Stokes grumbled from up front. "Like the ma'am said, be ready to run like hell… And you better not try playing grab ass in there. Get yourself popped for misconduct, and I will straight up whoop your ass." He looked back past Evan. "Sorry, Ma'am. This one's a little squirrely."

"It's alright Sergeant." She smiled; her hand rested on Evan's shoulder.

Evan stepped up to the first station, a woman in full hazmat gear, with doubled-up nitrile gloves. She didn't have on the usual protective mask, rather a full-face shield fixed to the seams of her hood. "What're you testing for?" he asked.

Silence, as she grabbed his finger and pricked the tip, collecting the blood sample in a narrow plastic tube; she slipped it inside a blue and grey plastic machine.

"Hello?" He stared at her vacant expression, not expecting an answer. "And what's that machine do?"

She pressed a button; the LCD display showed a status bar moving steadily along, then beeped. "Clear," she announced. "Next!"

Evan looked up along the scaffolding built along the ceiling and noticed a rifle aimed at him. He looked back at Captain Arden, hoping that whatever they were looking for, they wouldn't find.

Inside the painfully lit tunnel was a series of chambers. A strong smell of concentrated vinegar hit him at once, emanating from a basin at the center of the first chamber; diamond plate metal steps on either side of the trough. He stared down into the clear liquid for a while, a taped red line continued down into the basin, yet the red had faded to white. He dipped down slowly, only the tip of his toe touching the cold solution. A sharp pain shot through his backside. He spun, dropping into the pool, his feet now fully submerged in the liquid. "Did you just…"

"I'm naked… in a closed room… with a bunch of guys." Despite a sly, sort of playful look in her eyes, her tone, the embarrassed manner in which she covered herself suggested more warning than flirtation. "Hurry the hell up."

He stared, part shock, part embarrassment, and perhaps a smidge of excitement. Clamping his eyes closed, he whispered, "Sorry," then turned and walked through to the other side. As he emerged from the solution, a clear dividing line of bleach white, contrast his normally tannish skin tone. Partitioned with a plastic sheet, the second chamber was laid out with a set of two pipes, three feet apart at their closest, each sprayer oriented at a 45-degree angle, an eye-watering substance shot a fine mist from each nozzle. The placard at the front showed an animated image raising their arms, the image of liquid spraying beneath each armpit. "Idiot proof," he mumbled.

Awkwardness still gripped him, and for the next several chambers, he avoided looking back

Each chamber appeared to be some new configuration, or new solution. He had gone through chemical training, taken chemistry in high school and college, and this was nowhere near a standard decontamination.

As he reached the final chamber, the same sharp, cringeworthy smell as the first chamber hit him again, a thought clicked in his head; something he had read about, something he had smelled first hand at the dairy farms back home. Sergeant First Class Stokes stepped up into the chamber, and Evan felt the sudden urge to grab him, yet his feet remained planted. He watched the agents, fully garbed in hazmat suits, cover him head to toe in the pungent substance, and he realized, *they don't know the virus they're trying to kill.* He felt an arm brush against his back.

"You ok?" Captain Arden whispered.

Without looking, he turned his head slightly and nodded.

"Sorry about… you know," she whispered. "Thought I was being funny."

Silent and blushing, he smiled bigger.

Had he looked, he would have seen her blushing as well, yet more ashamed than embarrassed as she stared down at the floor.

"Sorry about staring."

"Hmm?" Her head shot up.

"For staring," he looked back at her, his eyes fixated on hers, trying desperately to mirror the same foreign kindness in his own. "You know, cause you're naked… in a room… with a bunch of guys."

She let out a slight giggle. "You say that, like- "

"Step forward." An agent motioned with his hand. He pointed downward to two placards, the first of a face, showing the eyes closed and mouth shut, the second of a body position, legs spread, arms held out at the sides. "Don't inhale!" the words muffled through his chemical mask

He felt the cold mist against his skin, an instant burning, as he tried desperately not to breath. Then final relief as the mist turned to water, flushing the chemical from his skin. He looked down at his arms, no longer a light tan, but coarse and white with a hardened layer of dead skin cells. On the other side was an open atrium at the head of the concourse, rows of tables aligned by size. Out of nowhere, he felt a jab in his arm, a loud hiss, as a foreign substance shot painfully into his muscle. He nearly reared back and punched the agent in the face, but given the likelihood of being shot, he decided against it.

The agents manning the tables wore only white paper masks; their unmarked, black fatigues and MP5 rifles suggested some sort of government agency. He eyed one curiously at one of the many long tables. "So, what's going on here?"

As though mechanical, the agent yelled back, "Dress at the benches provided," his hand extended down the row towards a large industrial light mounted on a tripod, illuminating the deadened hallway, airport shops and restaurants sealed off with metal gates. "move along to the security checkpoint to receive your personal effects."

He spotted Captain Arden from down the row towards an adjacent table, quickly tied his new boots and walked her way. "We need to talk," he whispered, extending his hand to her.

She looked up, wide eyed.

"Huh?" Evan looked around in surprise

"You should see your hair." Captain Arden reached over towards her own, and gasped, the chemical had turned it to a shade of burnt orange; she huffed. "What is it?" She stared up at him with a frustrated look and grabbed his hand.

"I was thinking about it while we were in there. Cellphones are ground based." He started towards the temporary security checkpoint set up an alcove alongside the tramway. "Not to mention, a nuclear detonation wouldn't actually cripple the comms infrastructure. It's not radiation they're worried about."

She stared at him with a puzzled look. "And?"

"Whatever they just decontaminated us for, it's biological." He walked up to a TSA agent at the checkpoint, handing out bins full of soggy, chemical-laden personal effects, the contents of which seemed mostly ruined. "Staff Sergeant Evan Decker," he announced to the agent.

"Captain Lindsey Arden." She watched as the single agent searched through a battalion's worth of personal effects. "How do you know?" she whispered.

"Three things where I'm from; mines, cash crop and dairy. Worked all three for a time. That smell... same stuff used to clean the milk holding tanks. Peracetic acid, kills all biological material."

The agent dropped a bin on the table. She shuddered at the sight of her few belongings floating in the foul solution. She tore her hard-plastic laptop case from the pool, pulled the computer out. "Oh, thank God," she whispered, a sigh of relief at the dry contents inside.

"Pretty attached, I take it?"

"You fight with guns." She glanced up along the second level, then at the ground floor exits, each guarded by an armed agent. "This is my gun."

They stepped inside of the tram, packed to the gills with nervous Soldiers, rifling through the contents of their assault packs, hoping for some shred of their belongings intact. Most found damaged laptops and cellphones, photos, images worn white, small keepsakes and religious medallions with their gold and silver veneer pitted and peeled off. "Stick close by me," she whispered, "If you can."

The tram moved slower than Evan remembered. *Degraded power?* he wondered. He made a mental inventory: power loss, biological decontamination, security by a federal agency – *but why not the national guard, and why full body suits and respirators? Is it airborne? Doesn't explain the power outage.* His thoughts were interrupted by the screeching breaks.

Captain Arden nudged him in the side.

A line of guards stood outside of the tramway at one of the domestic concourses, a horde of people behind them, wearing paper surgical gowns.

"Look at their feet," she whispered.

Bleached white, like the rest of them, but the attire was different. Jeans went from blue to bone white at the calf, athletic pants with holes worn at the fringes, yet he wondered what they had done with their shoes.

"Civilians," Captain Arden mumbled.

The tram stopped at the main terminal, a cadre of agents awaiting their arrival. As they stepped out, a voice forward of them shouted, "Someone want to tell us what the hell's going on here?"

A large armed agent stepped in through the mass of Soldiers, his arms like steel pipes. Evan fixated on his sleeves rolled up over giant forearms, as he gripped the unwitting Soldier and threw him forward, flat on his face towards the staircase. "Move out!" the agent shouted in a thick gravelly voice. A large opening formed around him and everyone moved towards the staircase, like a river around a boulder.

"Seen your commander?" Captain Arden whispered, moving steady along with the herd.

"Not yet." They walked up the dimly lit escalators, towards the light. "Maybe they picked him out of the group."

"Haven't seen Colonel Trajan, either," she whispered, as the herd moved forward into the large atrium of the main terminal, sparsely lit with sunlight and the few temporary light fixtures posted around the perimeter. "I'm starting to feel left out."

From his last return trip from the middle east, Evan remembered the decorative light fixtures lining the open three-story structure; a bustling metropolis of both travelers and USO volunteers stood anxiously along a partition, cheering at their arrival home. There were partitions now, meant to keep them corralled, more armed agents were posted at the exits, a man stood atop the second level staring down at them. Different from the others, he wore a wrinkled black suit and a white collared shirt, now yellowed, as though he had been wearing the same clothes for several days. His eyes were strained, tired looking.

The agent waited, as they all filtered into the room. "No doubt you have questions." His words seemed rehearsed, as though he'd done this, many times over. "Our president, in the last executive order of his administration, has recalled all troops from overseas. Over the last three days, our country, as you know it, has changed. An unknown enemy has executed a complex attack, beginning with a widespread communications blackout, biological attack of an unknown virus, whose delivery system is unknown…" He paused, seemingly overcome with genuine emotion. "Originating in Washington D.C. Millions are dead."

A shared gasp went out among the room, silence, then murmurs.

Captain Arden leaned in and whispered, "Wonder which senator didn't show up to work that day."

"You think it's domestic?" Evan whispered back.

She shrugged.

"Our task," the agent continued. "is that our nation survives, no matter the cost. Not only must we secure our borders, but our population as well. 2-25th Air Assault Battalion is assigned to…" he stared down at his clip board. "Fort Carson, Colorado."

The murmurs grew, as a collective gripe went out across the battalion, as that put many of the Soldiers a solid 800 miles from home in Fort Hood, Texas. Evan didn't care, as he didn't really have a home, nor anyone waiting for him. Aside from his car, securely held in storage, there were no possessions that were so dear as to worry about losing, and the car was questionable.

The agent motioned with his hands, "Quiet down... I can assure you that our office will do its very best to notify your next of kin that you've arrived safely, and return you home once your tour of duty here is done."

"What office?" A voice in front yelled. "Who are you? Who do you work for?" Captain Arden recognized the voice as Lieutenant Fellows, a platoon leader in Company A. "And what do you mean the president's *last executive order*?"

"And where's Lieutenant Colonel Trajan," Captain Arden yelled. "and all the company commanders?"

"Who's attacked us?" The room erupted in voices; the general unease now palpable. "Have they reached American soil?" "We've been gone a year and a half, when the hell do we get to go home?"

"Relax, everyone," the agent yelled, an anxious nerve struck in his voice. "Relax. Most of your questions I can't answer. Nothing has happened to your commanders; they're being briefed on the contingency plan specifics. And my apologies, I'm Agent Jacobs,

Department of Homeland Security. You'll move out to the front entrance, busses will be- "

"Maybe put that at the beginning of your little speech," Captain Arden yelled. "And better yet, maybe tell us what the hell's going on right when we get off the plane!"

Agent Jacobs let out a frustrated sigh, visibly shaken at the critique. "I'll keep that in mind… Barring any questions, please move out to your busses at the front."

Evan looked over at her, his eyes wide with a shocked grin.

"And what about Washington?" Captain Arden yelled. "Tell us what happened."

Jacobs stopped, his eyes dead set on her. "The President's dead… Washington D.C. has fallen."

"To who?" she yelled back.

His eyes widened. "I don't know."

CHAPTER 3

L eaving the airport seemed oddly reminiscent to going outside the wire of a combat outpost. Once clear of the entry control point, then the police barrier on either side of the surface streets, the scene looked more akin to Falluja or Mogadishu than suburban Atlanta - cars turned up on their sides in fighting positions, buildings smoldering near and far, pock marked asphalt where large caliber bullets had impacted and explosives detonated, leaving smeared remnants of human carnage on the street. From behind a ridge in the distance, black plumes of smoke rose; the hint of a kerosene fire. Evan wondered if they were burning the bodies there.

Evan peeked out from the third row towards the front of the bus. "Hey, boss," he said to the lone agent standing tall at the front, his foot cocked up onto a riser. "What happened here?"

The agent looked down over dark aviator glasses, holding the butt of his rifle against his hip. "War."

"Hah!" Evan muted a chuckle, while secretly wondering if the agent imagined himself as a warden transporting a bunch of prisoners. Still, he hadn't seen a service patch. Maybe this guy was a U.S. Marshall. "Who won?"

"You're a *smart guy.*" The agent pushed his sun glasses up on his face. "Aren't ya?"

"Takin' it off here, Boss," Evan drawled sarcastically with a deep southern twang in his voice.

Captain Arden leaned over into the aisle, one hand pressed against Evan's thigh, the other motioned outward dismissively. "Forgive my Soldier… He's a combat arms guy, and not a very smart one." She smiled wide and candidly, waiting until the agent huffed and turned back to his incessant pacing, then she turned back to Evan. "Seriously! Will you shut the hell up, before you get yourself shot? That's twice now."

Evan shrugged. "I just…"

She let out a frustrated sigh. "Listen, Cool Hand Luke." She smiled her familiar, endearing smile. "To be fair, it was a little funny."

"Are you psychic or something?" He breathed heavy, an odd sensation building in his chest. "Or just good with old movies?"

"Worse." Her eyes narrowed, as she shrunk secretively. "Women's intuition… and maybe I like young Paul Newman without a shirt. Funny, you remind me of him a little." She glanced up and down the length of him.

His eyes widened, as he remembered something he had wanted to say. "This is gonna come off as super creepy… please, try not to take it as creepy."

"You're creepy." She smirked. "Got it."

"Whatever." He rolled his eyes. "You remind me a little of- "

A gasp came from their side of the bus, their eyes shifted immediately out the window; a passing glance of four people on their knees, hands clasped behind their heads, another slumped face first on the ground, a pool of blood growing wide across the concrete. Two uniformed Soldiers, weapons drawn, aimed at those on their knees.

"Holy shit," Captain Arden mumbled.

A hand touched him from between the seats; his body clenched in fear. Staring back, only a single eye and dark skin were visible, hunkered down below the seat. "Cover me," Stokes whispered.

"What?" Evan whispered. "Where you going?"

"You see that shit?" Stokes whispered. "Captain Sayyid and First Sergeant are at the back of the bus. Keep the agent busy."

"There's a problem." Evan looked up tentatively at the agent, vigilantly standing at the head of the bus. "He doesn't like me."

Stokes put his palm to his face.

"For the love of…" Captain Arden mumbled, throwing her leg over Evan. "I'll do it." She looked back, now seated on Evan's lap. "Don't enjoy this too much," she whispered.

"What the hell?" he mumbled, watching her walk up invitingly towards the agent. "Is she… flirting with me?"

Stokes reached in again from between the seats and grabbed Evan's shoulder. "For a college boy, you're not real smart, are you?" He waited until the agent's shoulder turned, then walked back passively towards the bus lavatory.

They would come to find out that sitting in the back of the bus, Captain Sayyid had said very little, only, "There's not enough information yet to make a decision."

"Coward," Evan called him.

Sayyid was of Middle-Eastern descent, only one generation removed from Kuwait. He once had the opportunity to return, reclaim his right to oil of his family, gradually pumping towards an empty well.

What a strange man, Evan thought of Sayyid. *Reject your family and fortune in Kuwaiti oil to become an atheist, and an Army officer.*

"The women are better looking over here," Sayyid joked, yet his eyes were open to the world, the noose of unsustainable resources, of an unsustainable geopolitical system, of the lies told by government officials and religious leaders. Sitting at the rear of the bus, his eyes showed fear, as he would be the one tightening the noose around his country's neck.

Evan hated the man, short sighted and often toxic, misogynistic – even by Evan's standards, and what sealed it, the man had a family who by all accounts loved him, yet Sayyid ran from them.

What Evan would've given for his family to be whole again?

As Evan sat idle, he felt an odd sense come over him, now powerless. In that moment, his father's assessment of him had finally come true. He was *useless*, and *what use would the military have for a worthless nothing*, like Evan? Part of him hated his father, Samuel. Something had changed in the man, turned him sour, ever since… A memory bubbled up to the surface, too painful to think about, then subsequently stuffed back down into Evan's psyche.

He looked down at his hands, no weapon to fight with, no tools to build with, not even so much as a knife or wire cutters – not that there are many IED's planted along American highways. He'd done everything he could to prove Samuel wrong. He'd defied his father and joined the military, although not the Marines, as his father had; even made it to Staff Sergeant, the same rank as his father. He'd gone to college, just a few credits short of an engineering degree. And what was his father? Just a sheriff in a Podunk little town. Hell, he'd matched or surpassed his father in every way imaginable, yet his father's words stuck to him as though tattooed across his forehead.

Captain Arden sat back down far too soon, yet the plan seemed to have worked. She seemed to sense that something was off and dropped her head down, looking up into Evan's eyes fixed down at the ground.

He returned with a forced, painful smile. "I think you would've done better with some daisy dukes on."

She giggled softly. "What's wrong?"

Evan gritted his teeth and shook his head.

"I know." She smiled back, gently patting his hand. "It'll be ok."

"It's not that," he whispered. "I've seen much worse."

Her hand gripped tight around his, reminding him she was there. "Then what?" Her hands were soft, yet strong; just something he noticed, yet had no thought to consciously appreciate. No doubt she held the strength to wield a weapon, or the dexterity and skill to tear apart equipment and make it run, or the tenderness to comfort him, if he would only ask.

"Just home... stuff. Thinking about my parents."

"Oh." Her fingers ran gently over his, perhaps comforting, perhaps nervousness in knowing there was nothing she could say to assuage his fears. "If they're anything like you, I'm sure they'll be just fine. Tell me about them, and you. Where you from?"

Evan wondered how much of himself he should reveal. He was surely able to talk to women, though the difference in ranks threw him off, as did the prospect of candid conversation. His often-cocky attitude was a cover for fear; he knew that much, but there was more there – pain, weakness, betrayal, something… something he couldn't remember. His life back in Wyoming hadn't been so much a topic of discussion, as something to avoid. He spoke of his father only to his mother, and even that was a sore spot, as her constantly defending Samuel and smoothing things over proved infuriating at times. Nonetheless, he loved his mother, and under the circumstances worried about her safety. He wondered now if he still loved his father, deep down in some twisted recess of his mind. "Cowley," he whispered. "Wyoming."

She leaned in closer, staring into his eyes. "What're you thinking about?"

Evan hesitated. She looked into his eyes, though lost in some memory. "I remember a boulder out front of my house," he whispered. "Second house coming off the main road. My brother and I, we used to play king of the mountain on that boulder, and…"

Her eyes beckoned – *what else?*

He shuddered at the painful memories hovering just below the surface of his psyche. "Nah," he whispered. "What about you?"

She paused a moment, just sitting there, looking at him, holding his hand.

"I'm not interesting," Captain Arden whispered. "I'm a computer geek from Ohio, I have an ex-husband that hates my guts… He's an infantry type… not that that's a bad thing. He's just more… *misguided* than most."

Evan laughed. "That a nice way of saying he's crazy?"

"Yea." She giggled a bit. "Parents live in separate retirement communities down in Florida. So, you've never been married?"

He rolled his eyes at her attempts to pry. "Nope."

"That's alright," she said. "I don't recommend it."

Evan stared at her bashfully. "Was it that bad that you'd never consider it again?"

"Well, maybe." Her eyelashes fluttered. "Would have to be someone really special… I don't need any more assholes in my life. You're not an asshole, are you?"

He laughed. "Depends who you ask."

"Say I ask your ex-girlfriend?"

"Hah." His nose scrunched at the thought. "Maybe a little."

"I'm sure you'll be someone special," she whispered, leaning closer into him. "To someone."

He stared at her, studying her face, wanting desperately to brush the hair back around her ear, caress her cheek, press his lips delicately to hers. "I think you're alright, too."

Lindsey smiled through tired, jetlagged eyes. "Just alright?"

He smiled and squeezed her hand. "Tell me something good about you."

She yawned. "It's your turn. I've been doing all the talking."

"Hmm," he mumbled, trying to conjure an image of something positive. "I'm scared."

She held him tighter now and whispered, "me too."

$\sim$

The last thing he remembered was her head resting gently on his shoulder, as his eyes became heavy. The painkillers were wearing off and a dull throb started. His eyes opened to the desert, desolate mountains far off in the distance. Boulders and scrub-grass pock marked the land along the dirt road they were traveling. A call came out over the radio, "Atlas 1-1, this is Atlas 2-1," his friends voice, Staff Sergeant Bobby Don rang through static across the radio, garbled from the signal jammer, a Duke electronic warfare system. "We have a culvert approximately 200 meters ahead... Go do your thing."

"Copy that," Evan said back, staring down Bobby's lead MRAP armored vehicle 50 meters ahead.

He looked back at Private Hayes. "In 3… 2… 1" The doors swung open in sync. As if carefully choreographed, they both aimed their eyes and rifles down at the ground, then swept in bands out away from the MRAP armored vehicle. They stepped out with a crunch of dirt and rock, crouching down below the vehicle to look for IED's. Evan keyed the microphone fixed to his shoulder. "Clear." They shot out at a 20-degree angle, forward of the vehicle, stepping over stones and rutted ground from flash floods; a sweeping motion of their rifles in an imaginary box, side to side along the ground, then up along the embankment running along the road.

Evan knelt down, parallel with the corrugated steel pipe passing underneath the road; a blockage, maybe rocks, maybe garbage, then he saw it, an ant trail - buried wire leading up towards a rocky outcropping 300 meters away. He took another good look at the entrance of the culvert, a second ant trail leading out running parallel with the road. "Bobby," he transmitted. "Recommend you back the fuck up, secondary IED, hard wired." The air shifted.

"Crack!" The first round of a bolt action rifle ricocheted at the dirt around his feet, followed by the 'Clack, Clack, Clack,' of automatic weapon fire, the shriek of RPG's. Evan turned and sprinted towards the outcropping, bullets whizzing past his head. At first, he could hear it, then he felt the ground shake beneath his feet, the pressure and heat on his back, and he knew Bobby was dead.

Part of him didn't care anymore, standing exposed in the Afghani wasteland, his own life meant nothing now. He would find the trigger man and kill him, as warfare demands, but it wouldn't matter. Bobby didn't need to be here, and neither did Evan. Revenge would not be sweet, and perhaps Evan would die before he even made it there.

Machine guns fired from all directions, the sound of grenades impacting rapidly in the distance meant that someone in the convoy must be alive and fighting back.

Evan rounded the rocky outcropping and found a man in dirtied clothes, his face covered by a white and black shemagh, hunkering down against the boulders as though clinging for dear life. In the insurgent's eyes… no, the *man's*, not the animal he'd been conditioned to see them as, he found only fear - the same fear he had felt moments before Bobby died, the same fear he felt now, asleep on a bus headed towards Colorado.

Evan knew he was dreaming now, perhaps hallucinating from head trauma, he wished desperately for release from the nightmare, yet its grip forced his hand as the memory ran along its track. Thankfully, these were not the worst of his dreams. The barrel of the rifle aimed, no moral fiber would keep him from revenge, and then he fired.

Evan awoke in a shot. Lindsey's head still lay on his shoulder, her arms wrapped around his arm; what should have seemed like a pleasant moment was now clouded with uncertainty and loss, pain at his throbbing head. He wished his dreams could be untroubled; if only he could hold this very moment in his mind, discarding the past trauma. *What was it about this girl?* he wondered. *And what is it about me? I'm nothing. We're not in the same chain of command, but why risk it?*

"Sorry," Lindsey whispered, one final squeeze of his arm and she shifted back upright. "Thanks for the shoulder."

He stared at her with a puzzled look.

"Where are we?"

"I don't…" Evan realized that somehow his mind heard *what* instead of *where.* His eyes darted out the window. The sign read, 'Little Rock – 15 miles.' "Arkansas." His attention turned back towards her. "Seems a little like you're-"

"Listen," she said. "I don't want you to get the wrong idea. It's just amazing what you'll do when a gun's being pointed in your face, and some handsome guy tries to rescue you."

Evan half smirked. "So, I'm getting friend-zoned…"

She smiled; her hand lay on his forearm. "More like you're getting, 'I don't want to go to jail for fraternization' zoned."

His lips pursed and pride deflated, he nodded. Something so perfect was surely too good to be true.

"Not that I don't…" A conflicted look crept across her face, then shaken off like a sudden rain. "It's just better this way."

"Is it?" Evan looked out the window, trails of black smoke drifted into the sky.

"I don't know," Captain Arden mumbled, as the bus pulled off an exit ramp. A pile of rubble lay at the center of the underpass; burn marks along the edges where explosives had ignited. In the distance, a convoy of yellow school busses drove across an overpass, flanked on all sides by police cruisers.

Several steel mesh baskets sat along the incoming side of the road; a construction crew loaded chunks of concrete and boulders to fill the large barriers. Evan wondered whether the barriers were meant to keep people in, or out. He hoped for a moment that the occupants of the bus would be headed somewhere safe, however the prospects seemed unlikely.

Evan looked back down the aisle; a Soldier had been staring for the duration of the trip. "You know that guy?" he whispered.

Captain Arden peered over. "Specialist Sinclair. He's one of mine." She waved him over. "What's up?"

He stood there in the aisle, pressing uncomfortably against Evan. He had light brown hair, and his eyes seemed to say *I'm not all there upstairs.* "Mind if I have a word with you, Ma'am," he whispered. "Alone."

She looked up and down the length of the bus. "Think this is about as alone as we're gonna get."

Sinclair looked dismayed, like a child who's just been told 'no.'

Captain Arden motioned him closer. "Tell me." She looked over at Evan. "He can keep a secret."

"You don't understand, Ma'am." Sinclair looked down at Evan, sizing him up, as if he were somehow jealous. "I *know* what's happening."

Evan gritted his teeth, frustrated with the exchange. "So, spit it out, guy."

Sinclair's face soured, as if it were some great offense. "Some other time." He backed away slowly. "Sergeant, Ma'am."

Evan shook his head. "That was creepy."

She elbowed him playfully in the side. "No creepier than you."

CHAPTER 4

Attack aircraft soared off in the distance, along the backdrop of Pike's Peak and the Rocky Mountains of Fort Carson. Evan found it strange given the lack of communications on ground. *Maybe they've got a system worked out*, he thought. They pulled beside a tan, three-story, stone building; the unit crest was mounted on a placard alongside the road - a black dragon in front of a crusader's sword.

Both agents and Soldiers stood outside, wearing varying levels of biological protection; ready to greet them, rather hustle them off the busses. "Go, go, go!" an agent shouted, his face covered with a grey plastic mask, a pink particulate cartridge off either side.

Out on the lawn, another agent yelled, "Commanders and First Sergeant's, pick a spot, gather your units!"

Evan looked over at Captain Arden, a wishful longing in his eyes. "See ya."

"If things go bad," she whispered, then grabbed onto his collar and pulled in close. "I'll try to find you… Please be safe." She grabbed his hand and squeezed once more.

"Company A!" First Sergeant Baker yelled. "Form up on me!"

"Listen fellas…" Captain Sayyid stooped down on a green tough box. "They're not gonna let us leave."

An immediate roar of gripe and frustration issued from the troops. Evan sat at the back of the room, alongside another squad leader, Staff Sergeant Cass, silent.

"Fellas, shut the hell up!" Sayyid raised his hands, urging calm. "I'm not happy about it either. Hell, we've been gone 15 months. I'm anxious to spend time with my… well, away from you guys, anyway." A slight chuckle at the wise-ass comment; He shook his head and exhaled deep. "We're in a state of national emergency, fellas. Washington D.C. is gone. Zero comms, a full-on biological epidemic, tens of thousands dead, damn near full satellite degradation, blackouts, starvation, rioting."

The room quieted at the realization; the potential that loved ones could be impacted.

"I'm sorry," Sayyid whispered. "I wish I had better news." A large map appeared on the back screen of the briefing room. "We will conduct a tactical movement out as a Battalion towards the Brigade assembly area in the south of Denver, then occupy a company operations area in the northwest of the city," Sayyid said. "In order to- "

"What kind of biological epidemic?" Lieutenant Chilcot asked. He was a young punk from Detroit, all white-boy, with a smidge of Cherokee Indian and wet behind the ears, but many a hard lesson overseas and his blatant honesty had earned him respect. "What're we dealing with?"

Sayyid's eyes narrowed on him. Part of what had earned Chilcot respect was in candidly questioning orders that didn't make sense, out of the scope of good order and discipline, but necessary nonetheless. Sayyid gritted his teeth. "I don't know, but your squad is first up for the burn detail."

"And the comms outage?" Chilcot asked, unflinching, restraining a smug look on his face. "What's the cause?"

"Solar flares," Sayyid fired back.

"Oh." Chilcot nodded cynically. "That's the line of bullshit they're feeding you, Sir?"

Sayyid looked towards the back of the room, a solitary agent sitting with his arms folded. All eyes turned towards the back. The agent was a stout well-built man, his skin nearly blending with his black uniform, his eyes sharp, with a relaxed nature to his posture. He simply nodded without speaking.

Chilcot pointed his thumb back at the agent. "Who the fuck is this guy, Sir?"

"Quinn," the agent said. "Call me Quinn."

"Happy, Lieutenant?" Sayyid growled. "Any other burning questions?"

Chilcot raised his hands defensively. "Just making sure we're all on the same sheet of music, Sir."

He and Sayyid had a love hate relationship, as the Company's best, yet most obnoxious platoon leader.

Sayyid let out a frustrated sigh, and tugged down, straightening his top. "Our task is to- "

"Sir." Evan raised his hand. "Real quick."

Sayyid's lips pursed. "Go ahead, Sergeant."

"I saw they were using SINCGARS radios on our way in," Evan said. "Problem is, SINCGARS are ground based, just like cell. If cells don't work on account of solar flares, SINCGARS shouldn't either."

Sayyid raised an eyebrow. "What're you getting at, Sergeant?"

"Don't know, Sir." Evan shrugged. "Just that solar flares should be temporary at best, same as nuclear detonation. Doesn't make sense."

Sayyid's brow furrowed. He looked up at First Sergeant Baker. "Any idea, Top?"

"Military hardware is ruggedized." First Sergeant's face soured as his normal look, his voice was hard like granite, unforgiving. "Holds up better than that cheap civilian cellphone bullshit."

"I might just be a dumb EOD tech," Evan's eyes narrowed, he pulled his hands behind his back at parade rest, knowing he was right on the line of getting chewed out, pain shooting up the base of his spine. "Solar flares interfere with ground-based comms, they don't damage them. Hell, the whole idea of electromagnetic pulse or a nuclear detonation permanently damaging electrical systems and communications is garbage. Just sayin', this ain't the movies, and it takes a hell of a lot more to permanently disable comms."

First Sergeant crossed his arms with a condescending stare. "Sounds a little above your pay grade, Staff Sergeant."

Evan let out a long sigh. "I'd bet me electrical engineering degree on it, Top."

"This is some bullshit!" Staff Sergeant Cass rose. "You know it." He pointed at Captain Sayyid. "And you know it, Top. Quinn, whoever the fuck you are, you know it too."

First Sergeant's eye twitched. "Lock that shit up, Cass, Decker… and you too, L.T."

"And the epidemic?" The Executive Officer, First Lieutenant Jackson seated at the back raised his hand – 'Ass kisser,' the company often said of him. "You want us in full MOPP gear?" - A full chemical body suit and masks, cumbersome, hot and generally a pain to wear.

"Aww!" A collective gripe went out among the room. "C'mon!"

"Hold it down!" Sayyid motioned his hands downward. "Current level is MOPP Zero, you'll be issued particulate and biological filters for everyday wear. If you encounter infected, don masks, report up your position. Now can I get through this damn briefing!?" He paused a moment, ready to blast the next person who spoke. "Great... our tasks, perform missions associated with humanitarian assistance and sanitation. On order, perform counter-insurgency operations, and neutralize domestic enemy combatants."

Once more the room was in an uproar. "Enemy combatants?" Chilcot yelled. "You mean civili- "

"Ya'll shut the fuck up," Quinn yelled, as he rose and walked towards the front of the room. "Sorry to tell ya'll, this isn't the America you left. There're people out there... used the epidemic, the comms outage to their advantage. America... greatest nation in the world? We go dark for less than a week, and we've got our own version of Al-Qaida. So, either you're on board with this, or there's the door." He pulled out his pistol and racked the slide back. "Don't let the door hit you on the way out, cause my hollow point sure as hell will."

The room was silent.

"That's all," Sergeant First Class Baker said. "You're released to your Platoon... And Sergeant Stokes, come see me."

Moments later Sergeant stokes walked over to Evan, a grim look on his face. "You drew the short straw, Sergeant Decker. You and Hayes have Charge of Quarters tonight."

"Duty? Tonight?! Short straw my ass," Evan mumbled. "Just got hit with a damn artillery round."

"I don't think he cares," Stokes whispered.

A sharp elbow jabbed Evan in the ribs. "Sergeant!" The voice whispered.

"Sorry." Evan whipped his head around; a sharp pain and dizziness followed. "Must be jetlagged."

"No kidding." Hayes downed the rest of a Rip-it energy drink. "How's the head?"

"Eh." Evan stretched his arms above his head, looking around the new unit headquarters, an unremarkable building home to hallways full of blank office space. "Think I'll go for a walk." The space was mostly black, the hum of a generator outside illuminating the few lights that burned down the hallway. Around a corner, he heard a door click shut.

The stairwell echoed with the click of boots walking up towards the third floor. Evan waited for another click - the door closing at the top. He made his silent ascent, then stopped along the second floor and looked out the window. Nighttime duty seemed a blessing in disguise, as he watched the rest of his platoon nearly a mile away, garbed in hazmat gear stacking bodies onto a smoldering pile of human remnants. With each surge of kerosene dumped onto the pile, the flame flickered higher in the distance; a putrid scent of death hung heavy in the air. He shuddered, thankful for the reprieve, however brief, then continued silently up the stairs.

"It goes against everything we stand for," Sayyid mumbled, as Evan tiptoed towards the door. Inside the starkly lit room was a shadow of a man, his face gaunt and long, pale in the dim light, standing beside Captain Sayyid. Another two across the table, one he recognized as Colonel Trajan, who wrung his hands on the table. The other seemed to be in charge. *A General, probably*, Evan thought.

"That's unfortunate," the General whispered. Evan could see his silhouette nod subtly. He recognized the voice now, General Tracy, who'd given Evan a coin once, shaken his hand.

The gaunt man moved, almost imperceptibly; the garrote wrapped around Sayyid's neck. He kicked momentarily, his eyes rolled white into the back of his head, then his body went rigid.

As being choked to death goes, a blood choke is the easiest and least painful. Evan knew, and was confident that after about five seconds, Sayyid felt little to nothing. Part of Evan wished the pain would linger a moment longer, but no, he consciously put that thought away... It was wrong.

Evan didn't gasp, nor scream, nor tense. He was numb to that now, although it had piqued his defensive nature. Sayyid wasn't one that Evan would defend at his own peril, nothing against the guy, *another lie he told himself*, but three officers against one unarmed and injured NCO was a death sentence. Women, children, true friends... they were different, those he would defend. Deep down he felt a worry grip him, a brief sadness for Sayyid, as he didn't deserve this end, nor did any of his men, but now Evan focused on silence, stillness; he moved into an alcove and waited what seemed like an hour for them to leave the room.

He couldn't see, but heard what sounded like the crack and pop of cartilage and bone. He hunkered down as the three left the room, the gaunt one carrying an obviously heavy olive-drab duffle bag on his back.

Evan walked into the room and shone his flashlight around; a single drop of blood lay on the table, the seat still warm from where Sayyid sat. There would be no need to preserve the crime scene. He was sure that his statement would be meaningless, except to get him killed, and this crime would go unpunished.

Evan walked back down the hall to the CQ desk.

"There he is," Hayes yelled, standing at attention in front of the gaunt man, now without his duffle bag. His nametape read *Haegen*, his rank – *Captain*.

"Where you been, Sergeant?" His voice seemed eerily calm and soft, with a slight Boston accent, as though he might stab you in the throat with an ice pick a dozen times, then stuff your body in a freezer. His eyes were wide, unnaturally alert.

"Latrine, Sir." Evan stared straight into them, unflinching; yet, his anxiety, the ramped up beating of his heart told him a fight was coming.

Haegen leaned in uncomfortably close, nearly nose to nose, as if sizing up Evan's constitution.

Evan didn't move a muscle, yet part of him wanted to rear back and headbutt Haegen in the bridge of the nose; another part, the logical part, wanted to cut his losses and run like hell.

"Imagine what we'd do to an enlisted?" Haegen whispered, an unsettling supremacy to his voice.

"Not sure what you're talking about, Sir." Evan said, his eyes still fixed on Haegen's. "Do what?"

"Oh, Nothing." Haegen smiled a crooked grin, glancing back at Colonel Trajan. "I sort of like this one... takes a lot of balls to look someone in the eyes and lie right to their face."

Trajan tensed, his hand instinctively moving down towards his sidearm.

"Have a nice night, fella's..." Haegen smiled in earnest, cinching the duffel bag up onto his shoulders. "See you in the morning."

CHAPTER 5

Evan nodded off as they rode the LMTV troop carrier north, along highway 25 towards Denver.

"Rough night?" Stokes asked, seated on the bench opposite Evan.

"You wouldn't believe me if I told you."

Stokes shuffled across the floor, moving a private out of the way. "Try me."

"You're not gonna be seeing Captain Sayyid anymore," Evan whispered.

Stokes' brow furrowed as he drew back.

"He's dead."

Stokes lifted an eyebrow.

"Told you, you wouldn't believe me."

"And you saw it happen?" Stokes cocked a cynical gaze.

"Captain by the name of Haegen," Evan whispered. "Choked him out with 550 cord."

Stokes let out a long sigh. "We gotta get outa here, man."

"They won't let us," Evan said, his eyes now fixed out of the back of the troop carrier, a smoldering black mound, people gowned in white hazmat suits encircled it, spraying it with flames. The wind shifted, the scent of burning flesh and a familiar scent, similar to diesel or napalm, mixed with rotten meat. Evan's eyes watered; he looked back and others were vomiting in the back of the cargo hold. He looked back at the mound, now blazing orange up to its peak. It wasn't uncommon – burning diseased bodies, he could think of at least a handful of instances where incineration was the preferred method in dealing with the outcome of disaster, or outright genocide; Nazi Germany stood out. Inside, the pile of flesh was moving; parts breaking free, wriggling at the heat. It was then that Evan's stomach turned, a stark realization that within the mass of burnt flesh, people were still alive.

Objective Bronco, an apt name for the staging area in the south of Denver; The controlling element was a mix of both Army and Air Force Brigades and a half dozen other governmental organizations, who had set up shop at a high school sports complex, utilizing the open fields as helicopter landing zones. Adjacent to the complex was a large warehouse and concrete parking area; droves of Humvees lined up along parking spaces. Far off in the distance, the distinctive muzzle break of M777 artillery cannon rose high along single story neighborhood homes; its tube recoiled, sending steel downrange, followed immediately by tremors through the Earth. Evan felt at home here, yet *there could be nothing humanitarian about this*, he thought.

A mix of Soldiers and agents shuffled them in to an open warehouse bay, illuminated with sun and two harsh ultraviolet tripod lights. On the floor was a sand table, set up as the city of Denver. Streets were labelled and laid in matte black ribbon, rivers of blue yarn, buildings set up as blocks, detailed as meticulous as possible in depicting the operations area. Green and blue army men were set up along each axis of advance, depicted by an arrow, converging on the center of the city; A jagged line of brown army men as opposition. *Civilians,* Evan inferred. He noted where he had seen the pile of burning flesh, depicted with a triangle of paper, a flame at its center. Scanning the entirety of the massive sand table, he lost count at 20 such piles.

"Alpha Company!" an officer yelled, walking with purpose towards the head of the table. "I'm Major Phillips, Battalion Operations, hold questions to the end." He pointed down at the sand table with a stick, orienting everyone to the operation. "The northeast corner has received the heaviest casualties… That is your axis of advance. From Highway 70 to 40th avenue, you will sweep in zone; search all buildings, assist in evacuation of sick or wounded to a casualty collection point within the city, remove any contraband material, including weapons and ammunition, explosives or anything needed to mount an offensive. This is a quarantine situation, no one leaves; once you've entered the city, you must complete a full decontamination procedure prior to exit. A follow-on chemical unit will perform an extraction once your sweep in zone is complete."

"What is this, Sir?" One of Evan's team leaders, Sergeant Beaudry stood. "The virus they're all talking about."

"Like nothing we've ever seen before." The voice came from behind; an old lieutenant, likely a prior service enlisted, a medical patch on his arm, below a ranger tab. "Completely resistant to antibiotics, symptoms are high fever, nausea, sweating, vomiting, rash, painful blisters and ultimately death, 100% mortality rate if infected... I can tell you that it shares some characteristics with influenza, Ebola and norovirus, but is far more aggressive than all three."

"Is anyone immune, Sir?" Beaudry asked. "Or does it kill everyone?"

"Wish I had an answer for you." The lieutenant shook his head. "If you make it back, you'll be screened and decontaminated prior to entry. Good luck."

"Thanks, L.T." Another Major stepped up, astute looking with peppered grey hair and glasses. "Be on the lookout for the following high value targets." He handed a stack of papers around the company. "Primarily drug dealers; capitalized on the degraded of comms and biological outbreak, assembled criminal and civilian forces against us. Current location is unknown."

The photos were of criminal leaders from all different gangs of different races; Black men wearing blue or red, Hispanics with faces heavily tattooed, White men dirtied and disheveled with long hair and beards.

"Your battlespace is located within MS-13 territory; perhaps the most dangerous gang in existence.

Anticipate your target…" He looked out into the crowd for a specific picture. "You." He pointed at Evan to hold up the picture. "Victor Nunez will likely be the only High Value Target in your area of operation." He held the photo up, a man around age 35, shaved head, some tattoos on his neck, concealable by the collar of a button-down shirt, but otherwise normal looking. That wasn't what caught Evan's eye. Once a man sees combat, he looks different, like his eyes cast a little lower than before; like Nunez' photo, as Evan stared back, a mirror image.

"You're to shoot on site," Major Phillips interrupted. "I can assure you all, while this is our home soil and our enemy are American citizens, this is indeed war."

Sergeant First Class Stokes raised his hand. "Rules of engagement, Sir?"

Phillips paused a moment, his face unflinching, yet conflicted. "All non-military personnel with a weapon are considered combatants."

"Genocide," Evan mumbled, imperceptible to those around him.

A familiar face stood before them; Captain Arden handed off communications cards to Radio Operators in the Company. "We're experiencing localized and regional radio and digital interference," She blinked, then looked either way. "due to solar flares, as I'm sure you're all aware." She stared Evan in the eyes, blinked twice and her eyes shifted to the left.

"We've isolated open frequencies with minimal interference - noted on the cards, as well as Fire Support, Close Air Support and Medevac Frequencies." She blinked twice again, and shifted her eyes to the left.

'What the hell is she doing?' Evan wondered.

"Captain Haegen, First Sergeant Baker," Major Phillips said. "They're all yours, wheels up in 10."

"Move out!" First Sergeant Baker yelled; Huddled in tight, Soldiers scurried to get out of the cluster.

An arm reached out and grabbed Evan by the wrist. He felt Captain Arden's breath, hot along the ridge of his ear. "That's him. It's us," she whispered, as Evan was dragged along the ceaseless movement of bodies towards the exit. *Who's him? And what's us?* he wondered. *What the hell is that supposed to mean?* It was a shame she hadn't done something smooth like slipping him a note.

They marched around the side of the building, the side door was cracked only inches, but Evan could feel her presence, as he started for the door.

"C'mon, Romeo." Sergeant Stokes grabbed him by the arm, pulling him back in line towards the landing zone. "New commander's got his eye on you."

Evan shook his head, beyond frustrated.

ᴍ

They set up in the outfield of a baseball diamond. "Hope I get to use this thing." Private Hayes' ran his hands along the 12-gauge shotgun, loaded with bean bag ammo, his M4 slung around his back. The Company knelt in two even lines along a field, pointed outward for security – PZ posture.

Evan smacked him hard on the back of the helmet. "Watch your tone."

"I was just- "

"Shut it." Evan grabbed him by the chest plate. "These people are hungry, scared… We're not in Afghanistan, these aren't insurgents. You get me?"

Hayes shot him a bewildered look, as though unsure whether to lash out or make a smartass comment. "But the Major just-"

"Fuck the Major," Evan said, a hair too loud. "You follow me, do as I do, understand?"

Hayes looked over at Sergeant First Class Stokes, eavesdropping on the conversation. "Listen to him, Hayes. You don't shoot unless someone's a threat; you don't do anything to compromise yourself."

Hayes grit his teeth and nodded, then looked back at Captain Haegen. "What's with the new commander, where's Captain Sayyid?"

"Dead," Evan whispered. He looked back as Two Humvees pulled up to the rear of the formation. "That's Battalion commander, Division Commander too, looks like."

"What?!" Hayes whispered, looking back towards the Humvee's. "What're they – "

"Turn around." Evan grabbed him by the shoulder, ripping him back towards his sector of fire.

"What do you think they want?" Hayes whispered, stretching the pain out of his back. He had the unfortunate distinction of being the squad's radio operator, and carrying an extra 15 pounds in his kit.

"Don't know." Evan watched as Colonel Trajan handed off a piece of paper. "Probably just some bullshit." Haegen read through the page, nodding his head, line by line.

"What're they talking about," Hayes whispered.

Evan saw as General Terry and Captain Haegen slapped each other on the shoulders, as if congratulations were already in order. Colonel Trajan however, seemed out of place.

"A company man," Evan mumbled.

"Tell me what's going on," Hayes whispered

"Trust me Hayes," Evan whispered. "You don't want to know what I know, it's better this way… But I'll tell you this. Before I joined up, I spent a summer working in the mines back home, pissed my dad off something fierce… Every shift had 'em. The guy that keeps an ear out for union talk, defends the company to no end."

Hayes stared at him cockeyed.

"Don't trust the commander," Evan said. "he's a liar, and a killer."

A 'Thump, thump, thump,' of helicopter blades sounded faintly in the distance. "I am your new Commander!" Haegen yelled. "You may be wondering what happened to Captain Sayyid... While conducting reconnaissance last night, his convoy was unfortunately hit by enemy sniper fire. I am your replacement, my apologies for the lack of formality!"

"Bullshit," Evan muttered under his breath, the *thump, thump, thump*, growing steadily closer.

"Follow my orders," Haegen yelled. "And I can assure you I will make every attempt to get you out of this alive!"

"We shouldn't be here," Stokes whispered, *thump, thump, thump* now drowning out the commander. A wash of hot air shot out from the jet turbines; the back lift-gates opened on both chinook helicopters landing side by side.

Chilcot grinned. "At least with Captain Sayyid gone, no more burn detail."

Evan looked at him. "Captain Sayyid's dead, Sir."

Chilcot stared back, part disbelief, part shock, dismayed at his own words.

First Sergeant Baker stood at the front of the formation, pointing to his right, while signaling with his hands. "Headquarters, first and second platoon!" Then to his left. "Third, fourth and support platoon! Move out!"

Chinooks hovered over adjacent cross-streets; Evan zipped down the line dangling to the pavement below. Bullets whizzed by, nearly drown out by prop wash. He hit the ground and scrambled for the cover of a building.

Blood sprayed, a bullet entered a Soldiers neck and out through his throat. Evan hesitated, the body turned over, bleeding into a puddle on the pavement.

At the rate he was losing blood, there was nothing Evan could do for the young private. He dropped to his knees and held the young man's hand. It could be his older brother that he held there. Evan's sight clouded with rage, as the young man tried to mouth his final words. "Shhh." Evan put his finger over the young man's lips. "It'll be over soon."

The young man quieted, a persistent fear held in his eyes; twenty years old at best, only a boy. Evan could only guess at what he was thinking; perhaps his life flashing before his eyes, thinking of his family, wondering at an afterlife. Evan wanted desperately to save him now, helpless as he was – both the boy and himself.

"Why are we here?" he yelled, staring into the boy's dead eyes. He put his bloodied hands over the boy's face, shutting his eyes.

A roar of gunfire shook him back – the 'clack, clack, clack,' of a 240 Bravo machine gun firing only feet away. "Get the fuck over here!" Sergeant Stokes shouted. He hadn't heard that tone of voice since Sergeant Don died – bad memories stuffed back down at the incoming sniper fire.

Evan sprinted for the wall, past a lineup of downed vehicles; he slung his shotgun around his back and took up his rifle. Large caliber rounds pounded into the concrete barricade, a spray of debris at each impact. "Where's it coming from?"

"14th floor, open window, hiding behind the wall." Stokes looked down the line of Soldiers and found what he was after. "Hayes, your weapon." He grabbed it, and cracked open the grenade launcher fixed to the lower rail. "Ammo!" he yelled, as Hayes ripped off his bandoleer of grenades. Stokes flipped open the leaf sight and measured the wind at his back.

Evan looked down along the row of civilian vehicles, all oriented north, riddled with large .50 caliber holes, as if attempting to flee the city. "They wouldn't let them leave," he whispered.

"What's that?" Stokes yelled.

Evan shook his head, now staring down the impossible shot. "I said, no freaking way." It was a standard size window nearly a football field away. With a hollow 'plunk,' the grenade went sailing from the tube, and whether by sheer luck or deadly accuracy, landed squarely inside the window. From then on, the shooting stopped.

Stokes tossed the rifle back in a moment of bravado, seemingly pleased with his own prowess.

"That was an American," Evan mumbled.

Stokes grit his teeth, his nostrils flared into a snarl. "And an enemy sniper…"

Evan shook his head; soon he would have his own decision to make.

CHAPTER 6

They moved in bounding overwatch along the edges of the sidewalks, using the buildings and vehicles for cover. Along open spaces and roofs, through carnage and human remains smeared across pavement, mortars had pounded into the asphalt, leaving the ground pitted, debris scattered. A transmission came across Lieutenant Chilcot's radio, "Proceed to target location 1." He stopped behind another brick wall, the smoking remnants of a building, and brought out his map. To the rear, a team evacuated the fallen Soldiers body.

Chilcot pointed to a bombed out building adjacent to the target, "Overwatch!" A designated marksman hustled over and posted up behind a brick wall. "First squad, Move!"

Staff Sergeant Cass and his Soldiers rounded the corner and hauled ass towards the apartment building. The remaining squads followed suit, until the central lobby was filled with Soldiers.

"Squad leaders!" Chilcot yelled. "Fall in on me."

"I'm gonna say what we've all been thinking." Chilcot took a knee, the platoon leadership gathered around.

"That this is a bunch of bullshit, Sir?" Staff Sergeant Cass interrupted.

"You got it." He looked up at Cass with a sort of shocked indifference. "I was going to say that we're playing for the wrong team."

Sergeant Cass looked at him cross-eyed. "I don't swing that way, Sir."

Stokes smacked him in the helmet. "Shut the fuck up, Cass."

Chilcot shook his head. "We've been given orders in direct violation of the constitution… As an officer, I'm formally indemnified to act. As non-commissioned officers, so are you. We cannot in good conscience execute this mission."

"So, what?" Evan asked. "We just go guns blazing against a whole of division?"

"No…" Chilcot stooped his head down onto his fist. "But how we go forward will ultimately determine whether we're successful, and whether we go to jail or get shot once the dust settles."

"So, what?" Evan said. "We just wait it out? For what?"

"An opening," Chilcot said. "Then we run, defect, whatever you want to call it."

Evan shook his head, then looked over at Stokes. "You tell him?"

Stokes nodded.

"How do you feel about being a martyr?" Chilcot asked.

"So, let's say we wait for an opening." Evan folded his arms across his chest. "How many civilians am I gonna have to kill between now and then."

Chilcot rose. "And what would you suggest, Sergeant?"

"I say we frag the new commander, kill him, consolidate unit command under you and make our way back from where we came."

"No." Chilcot shook his head. "I can't legally support- "

"Since when do you give a shit about legality?" Evan said.

"When me going to jail or getting shot in the head for treason is on the line."

Evan gritted his teeth. His father was a sheriff. He knew damn well about legality was all about – the law takes down who it wants, when it wants, for whatever it wants, and if you weren't on the side of power, you were pretty well fucked. "I'll do it."

"No," Chilcot said. "If anyone were to do it, it would be- "

"You can say I acted alone."

"Stop," Chilcot yelled. "Enough of this. Even if you kill Haegen, what then?"

Evan cocked his head.

"Think they'll just let us turn around and walk out of here?"

"I…" Evan stuttered.

"They've got drones flying all over the city, strike capability up to 300k outside the city, close air support… we're gonna be fighting ourselves."

Evan grimaced. "What did you have in mind?"

"Play along…" Chilcot leaned in, whispering a plan that may just be insane enough to work.

Broken up by squad, each assigned a floor of an apartment high-rise, Evan knocked on the first of many doors on the second floor.

"Who is it?" a man's voice yelled through the door.

"Staff Sergeant Decker," Evan yelled back. "U.S. Army!"

"What do you want?" the door cracked open, the man's eyes peered back through dim candle light, dark as his skin.

"Just talk," Evan lowered his voice. "Answer a few questions and we'll be on our way."

The man glared back, his eyes dead set on Evan, just above the door chain. "So, talk."

"You have any weapons inside?"

The door slammed shut.

Evan grabbed the handle and turned, driving his shoulder into the door; a 'crack,' as the chain ripped from the wall.

Driven back, the man reached behind his back; an inexpensive Taurus compact, 9 mil pistol.

"Relax." Evan motioned with his hands, urging calm. "We don't want to take your- "

'Boom!' The shotgun blast, deafening, reverberated through the tiny apartment.

Evan dove for the weapon, his ears ringing. Two elementary age children huddled to their mother on the couch. "Hey, hey," Evan whispered, the children now sobbing. "It'll be ok." He moved to the man, now curled into a fetal position, holding his stomach. "You'll be alright, was just a bean bag round."

"Don't hurt my family," the man strained, tears coming from his eyes.

Evan looked up at Hayes, the barrel of his shotgun still smoking. "We're not here to hurt anyone." He grabbed the man under the arm, pulled him to a seated position. "Listen carefully," Evan whispered. "You need to hide your weapons. Somewhere no one would think to look… air vents, inside random objects. Not in the dresser or a safe or a closet. Second, don't bring it out unless you absolutely have to, understand?"

The man nodded, still trembling from pain.

Evan looked around the room. "Everyone else ok in here?"

The woman nodded; her arms wrapped tightly around her children.

"C'mon." Evan walked out of the room after Hayes.

"You're welcome." His tone sarcastic.

Evan grabbed him by the chest plate, slammed him into the wall. "You pull some crap like that again... Boy, I'll- "

A team leader, Sergeant Beaudry, grabbed on to Evan. "Let it go," he whispered.

Evan shucked his grasp. "Let's get this over with." He walked to the next door and knocked. "Staff Sergeant Decker, U.S. Army. Random health inspection."

The door cracked open, a young woman on the other side. "Why the gunshot?" she whispered in broken English.

"Just a misunderstanding." Evan smiled. "May we come in?"

"Dude pulled a gun on us," Hayes yelled.

"You," Evan glared back at him. "Stay in the hall."

The woman unclasped the door chain and swung the door open, shotgun in hand. "Insurance."

Her voice meek, the weapon too big for her petite frame.

"Good." He nodded. "Hide it, somewhere inconspicuous… don't take it out unless you need it or let anyone take it."

The weapon lowered, a confused look on her face.

"That's all." He started for the door. "Have a nice day."

Evan knocked on the third door down. No answer. He knocked once more. Nothing.

Hayes pressed forward through the squad, and knelt at the door. Evan's brow furrowed as he looked down. Hayes inserted two small tools into the lock, fishing for tumblers; a metallic 'click,' as the deadbolt turned open.

"I'm a little worried that you know how to do that," Evan mumbled, pushing the door open; stopped dead at the door chain. He motioned the breech man forward, battering ram at the ready. "No." Evan spun him a round, digging through his assault pack. The bolt cutters slipped in through, cut the chain cleanly. The apartment pitch black; Evan raised his hand, moved it back and forth sideways – tactical entry.

The squad stacked behind him. A tap on his shoulder and he burst through the entry, moving parallel down the adjacent wall, scanning his sector of fire – empty. He swung his muzzle into the bathroom, open, empty, then moved to the next door. The squad stacked and entered; two bodies lay side by side on the bed, a note laying below their hands joined in the middle.

Evan scanned the room, the bodies; an elderly couple dressed in their Sunday finest, tranquil in death. He picked up the note, messy handwriting, as if the author's hands were shaking.

Dear Brian,

We pray every day that you're well. We're sorry that you're finding us this way. We've dressed as to hopefully maintain some dignity in death, lessen the impact at your discovery. Our medication and food stores are exhausted, neither your mother or I have eaten in days, and she's fallen ill. Two days ago, Soldiers came, or what looked like them, handing out water. Besides that, there's been nothing. It's too dangerous out on the streets and this seems inevitable. May God have mercy on our souls, and hopefully he'll understand our decision.

Son, you should know how much we love you and hope...

"Shit," Evan whispered. "Infected."

"Gas, gas, gas!" Beaudry yelled, pumping his fists in an out to his helmet; the signal – '*put your mask on.*'

Evan put down the letter, now thinking of his own parents. His last words via text, 'call in a bit.'

Sudden regret, as he fit the gas mask over his face. He pulled a pair of nitrile gloves from his first aid kit, folded down the wife's collar; fever blisters had broken open on her skin, oozing a thick pinkish substance – likely a combination of puss and blood. He looked closer at the lips, lifted them with the tip of his knife, purple streaks had formed along the capillaries in the mouth. "Jesus," Evan whispered. He promptly sprayed down his gloved hands and his knife with a solution of the same potent sanitizer they had gone through at the airport.

"Check this out!" Hayes voice muffled through his mask. He stooped down inside the closet; a veritable arsenal of rifles and pistols lined up along the ground.

"You know," Beaudry mumbled, walking slowly towards the closet. "New commander's gonna be pretty pissed if we come back empty handed."

"Hm," Evan mulled the thought over. "Take it all."

"Don't know, Sir." Chilcot had his best poker face on, as Evan exited the building. "Still have two squads searching, but we're coming up with a whole lot of nothin'."

"You should know, L.T." Haegen's face tightened, a visible rage in his sinuous features. "There's plenty of other young officers in line." He gripped Chilcot's shoulder. "You're expendable." His words a threatening, malicious whispered. "Understand?"

"Roger, Sir." Chilcot remained straight faced, despite the tension. "We'll keep- "

"Hey, Sir!" Evan yelled, now walking with purpose towards the center of the street. "Take a peek." Soldiers to his rear, rifles and pistols stacked across their arms, up to their chests.

Haegen smiled a twisted, bony grin, then slapped Chilcot on the back.

"Where the fuck did those come from?" Chilcot whispered, as Captain Haegen and Agent Quinn inspected the haul.

Evan shrugged. "They were dead, Sir."

"You there, Sergeant Decker." Haegen motioned for Evan to come forward. "Come walk with me. Let's have a chat."

Reluctantly, Evan followed. He wished his meds weren't slowly wearing off. "Roger, Sir."

"I've talked to First Sergeant about you at length." Haegen put his arm around Evan's shoulder. "I know what you saw, and I know you hated Captain Sayyid… no doubt you've told most of your squad, probably the Lieutenant Chilcot, too. That's not what upsets me."

Evan hesitantly nodded. "And what bothers you, then, Sir?"

Haegen looked back, making sure that the rest of the unit was out of earshot. "That you might think I'm wrong for doing it."

Evan raised his eyebrow. *How could he imagine himself as right?* Then it dawned on him, and Haegen could see that it dawned on him, as he said, "I'm a Soldier, I kill that which is a threat. That's my job, my role, my only reason for existing, is to kill."

Evan cocked his head. "Our own people, Sir? Civilians?"

"Right is only a perspective," Haegen whispered. "These civilians, those in our Army that don't understand or don't agree with what we do. They are the enemy." He stared deep into Evan's eyes. "I think you understand that, don't you?"

Once more, he reluctantly nodded. He knew better than most, to what length the enemy would go to kill him, and to what length he would go to kill the enemy. Maybe Haegen was right.

"By the end of this," Haegen whispered. "You will understand."

Midnight, two large apartment buildings were cleared along the outside of the city, countless more to go. Alpha Company set up a hasty defensive position within the confines of an abandoned grocery store at the corner. Marksmen and forward observers set up on the roof, watching the two crossroads for movement. Evan lay dozing along aisle 2, his head propped up by a roll of paper towel. An occasional 'clack, clack, clack,' of automatic weapons, a 'crack,' from the sniper rifle shot out from up above, then a 'pop, pop, pop,' returned towards them, the incoming rounds penetrating the glass grocery store windows.

"You think we'll make it through this?" Hayes asked.

"Probably not," Evan said. "Just don't get sick or shot."

Hayes grimaced. "You're not worried about getting infected?"

"Nah," Evan stared up at the ceiling. "Figured when it's my time, it's my time." An odd thought occurred to him. "Hey, isn't there an Airforce base in Denver? Where are they?"

"When it's your time, it's your time." Agent Quinn laughed mockingly down the aisle. "They're dead… all of 'em."

"What'chu know about that, Narc?" Hayes asked, throwing on a thick urban accent. "That is what you are, right? DEA, CIA, FBI."

"I was a Marine, once upon a time." Quinn laughed once more. "As for now… you don't follow the news, do you, son?

Hayes looked at him cockeyed.

"I'll bring you up to speed." Quinn smiled sarcastically. "While you all were gone, congress in their infinite wisdom decided to gut the Department of Justice."

Evan felt his pockets. "Wonder if this place has a pharmacy," he mumbled. As badly as he wanted to engage in the political discourse, he knew what would come for him if he didn't act.

Walking towards the back of the store, bullets cracked through the plate glass windows along the top of the concrete structure, whizzing over his head in rapid succession. Automatic weapons echoed an answer from guards posted around the building. Evan felt a damp sensation along the back of his neck and reached back. He wondered whether his time might be up, a cheated feeling at the discovery of a ruptured glass bottle on the top shelf.

From the customer service counter, the pharmacy area was dimly lit in green with chemical lights. Someone was in there. He jiggled the handle – locked. The steel gate had been wrenched open; no doubt looted during the initial riots. He crept over the counter; a murmur of voices.

"Your disposition at our current situation, First Sergeant," Haegen whispered. "What're your thoughts?"

"It's good," First Sergeant Baker whispered back. "Establish martial law, get all these civilians under control and- "

"Hey, Top, Sir," Evan interrupted, now walking towards them. "Need something for my arm."

First Sergeant Baker rose, a hint of ire at the intrusion, and at the Soldier now looking for pain killers.

Evan aimed his flashlight down at the Captain's hand and shook it, as he hadn't had the chance before. His father had told him once, in one of the few pieces of good information he had ever passed on, *"Doesn't matter a man's occupation, you can tell a lot by his handshake. Whether he does his own work, whether he looks you in the eyes, whether he's a fighter, or a coward."*

Evan had long made it his practice of a firm handshake, solid eye contact, but then he'd look down at a man's hand and see what he was made of. A sudden impulse shot through Evan, a subconscious memory, a pattern. It was nearly imperceptible, like the ant trail leading out of the culvert, the disturbed earth hiding something deadly. His eyes fixated on the shape imprinted in the crux between forefinger and thumb– oblong like a football or an eye, no longer than an eighth inch; possibly a scar or burn, a faded tattoo or even a birth mark. "No," Evan whispered.

"What's that?" Haegen pressed.

Evan remembered General Tracy, the very same shape in the very same spot. "Nothing, Sir." He finally let go of Haegen's hand.

"Suppose it's alright." First Sergeant put his hand up. "He took some shrapnel to the arm. Had the chance to go home, but didn't."

Haegen smiled. "Why is that, Sergeant Decker?"

Evan rifled through white boxes with tiny print, his red lens flashlight sticking out of his mouth towards the racks. "Guess I couldn't get enough of killin'…" he garbled. "Sir."

Haegen smiled thinly. Evan wondered at whether he had seen any real combat. Likely, given their previous encounter. Though Haegen didn't have the same downward glare, rather a dangerous and malevolent look in Evan's assessment. He wondered once more whether they were the least bit similar, as he had been so eager to kill the triggerman that ended his friend's life. What was Haegen's stake in all this, he wondered?

"Bingo," Evan mumbled, pocketing all eight blister packs of Norco. His eyes widened when he realized there were four more boxes sitting just behind the one. "Evening, gentlemen." He nodded, shamelessly cradling his haul towards the exit. He stopped and turned to Haegen. "I do have one question, Sir."

Haegen raised his eyes to meet Evan's.

"What'd it cost you?"

Haegen's lips pursed as he pondered the question. Finally speaking, there could be no mistake of his conviction, he said, "Complete and total obedience."

Could I ever be that way? Evan wondered, the question clear on his face.

"What would you do if they ever ran out of those?" Haegen pointed to the boxes of pills swaddled up in Evan's arms.

Evan's brow furrowed; he didn't know. Perhaps one day he'd slay that demon, but not now, not yet. He crossed back through the steel mesh and plopped down beside Hayes; his fingers nimble in popping the blister packs into an empty medication bottle. "What'd I miss?" He stared down at Quinn, who lay on his side covered with a poncho liner.

"Something about Merging the CIA and NSA and all the other defense intelligence into one Federal Intelligence Agency, then the DEA, FBI, DHS and ATF into the Federal Police Agency," Hayes said.

"Damn, son." Evan popped open another box of narcotics. "A lot of letters there."

Hayes shrugged and rolled his eyes a bit. "Apparently the FIA runs the show. FPA are more like enforcers. Oh, yea." Hayes reached into his pocket. "I got this for you."

"The hell am I gonna do with this?" Evan examined the cheap burner phone, touchscreen with a decent camera.

Hayes shrugged. "Couldn't hurt."

"And what's our friend over there?" Evan noticed a slight movement under the poncho liner. "Hey, Quinn… hand check."

"Man, fuck ya'll." Quinn turned, the hint of screen light breaking through to the darkened room. "Think you know what the fuck's goin' on. Don't have a damn clue."

"Yea?" Evan downed a pill with water from his camelback.

Quinn shook his head. "You're not nearly as scared as you should- "

"Tell you what you should be scared of." Captain Haegen walked steadily, yet stealthily, so much that no one saw him coming. "A virus no one has ever seen before, an armed populace determined to overthrow our government, our way of life, everything we've worked for, fought for, died for."

"For them," Hayes mumbled.

"What's that, Private?" Haegen stared down at him, the fire in his eyes burning through, despite the dark.

"Nothing, Sir."

"No, no." Haegen inched closer. "I want to know, 'for them,' what?"

"We fought for them, Sir." Hayes gritted his teeth; he should have just shut up then and there. "For their right to decide their fate… you know, life and liberty, the pursuit of happiness?"

"What're you saying, Private?" Haegen's head cocked and eyes narrowed in examination. "You wouldn't sacrifice a few personal freedoms for security?"

Evan shook his head; it was too late now for Hayes to go back. "It's happened through history… never ended well."

Haegen smiled a malevolent grin, slowly shaking his head up and down. *Surely*, Evan thought, *he'll have Hayes killed when the time comes, just like Captain Sayyid.* "Do you know what happens to people that are unwilling to sacrifice what's necessary?"

"Don't know, Sir." Hayes closed his eyes. Evan expected a bullet any moment. "I just work here."

"Just work here…" Haegen chuckled; the nervous air in the room seemed to clear. "I'll accept that."

They waited as Haegen moved out of earshot. Finally, Quinn whispered, "You see his hand?"

Evan nodded his head.

"Just as you were talking, Hayes," Quinn looked down the row, checking once more. "You just about got shot."

Evan's brow furrowed, *at least it wasn't me this time*. More concerning, who was this government agent? And whose side was he on?

Hayes lit up a cigarette. "Lucky he doesn't get himself fragged."

"Quiet." Evan ripped the cigarette from Hayes mouth and mashed the growing red ember down onto the tile.

"The fuck?" Hayes looked at him sideways, as though ready to snap. "I know you didn't just- "

Evan pointed up towards a smoke detector, fixed beside a fire suppression nozzle. "I don't feel like getting rained on tonight."

Hayes stared, a bitter look on his face.

"Get some sleep, *Private*." Evan spit the word. "I'll take the radio." So seldom would he invoke his rank that it often seemed Hayes saw him as a peer instead of a superior... until Hayes stepped over the line.

Hayes whipped over, ripping his poncho liner over his shoulders.

Evan lay back, clipping the hand mic to his helmet straps. He shouldn't have fallen asleep, but he didn't really care. They couldn't do much to him now, except kill him. That wasn't reason enough, as the pain in his skull slowly subsided. If someone needed to get a hold of him, he'd hear the radio, or feel the toe of their boots kicking him in the ribs. Nothing to do now but let the world drift on by…

CHAPTER 7

Two hours into the night and the words, "Cool hand Luke," rang in his ear. "Cool hand Luke, this is Daisy Duke, do you copy?"

"You can't be serious." He rubbed the sleep from his eyes and clicked the hand mic. "This who I think it is?" he mumbled, still groggy.

"Yes," she whispered. "There's no time… Your boss is not on your team."

"Huh?" Shook his head, trying to comprehend. "What do you mean?"

"Your new boss is a traitor," Captain Arden whispered. "And there's more, many more. You need to kill him and get out. Go to the place- "

"Who's on the radio?" Captain Haegen yelled, storming down the aisleway. "Who the fuck is it?"

Evan drooped his head, pretending to be asleep. He felt a sharp jolt in his ribs.

"Get up!" Haegen yelled. "Shouldn't be sleeping. You the one talking on the radio… Cool hand Luke?"

Evan shook his head frantically, a glossed over stare in his eyes.

Haegen's face soured. "Shitbag," he yelled, kicking Hayes in the ribs. "Why you sleeping? Been talking on the radio?"

Evan breathed a sigh of relief; however, Captain Arden's voice was gone, with some key piece of information missing. He lay limp, pretending to nod off, waiting for a word.

Finally, Haegen's voice hissed through the radio. "Whoever's fuckin' around on my net... I will find you, and you will die. I promise."

Evan sensed a hard edge with the words, no idle threat, no lacking resolve. Whatever the stakes were here, they were much higher for Haegen, and likely higher for Evan, though he didn't yet realize it.

Another day, another patrol; more buildings to clear, more rights to suppress. Traveling along Larimer street, single shots rang out at a distance, large caliber. "Sniper, 1 O' Clock, 300 Meters!" The company scrambled for the cover of a wooden fence line, dotted with hedges, pinned against buildings and embankments.

Evan stayed in the open, scanning the buildings with his optics. Up many stories of an apartment complex, a window was broken out. He remembered the old green Battle Dress Uniform from pictures. When he joined it was the Army Combat Uniform digital camouflage. "Old camo," they called the greens, and now they were on to a brownish colored 'multi-cam.' The dark green patrol cap, flipped backwards was a dead giveaway. This guy was an old vet, and as Evan set his sights, so too did the vet. Somehow through time and space, through the waiting, they realized that neither wanted to fire.

The vet lowered his rifle, giving a slight nod to Evan, then retreated back into the building.

Evan shook his head. "I can't do this," he whispered.

"Where is he?" Captain Haegen yelled, propped behind a dirt embankment.

"He's gone." Evan lowered his rifle. "Probably egressed back to the main element."

"That means we're close." Haegen rose, brushing the dirt off himself. "Be prepared for significant enemy contact."

Evan wondered, in the oddest impulse, whether anyone would stop him if he shot Captain Haegen, right then and there. He was immediately disgusted at the urge. *Fragging an officer*, he thought. *That sort of thing doesn't happen anymore, does it?* Then again, the country hadn't been at civil war in over century and a half. For a moment, he wondered which side he was on.

He let out a long sigh, in the hopes that this too would pass.

It was a nasty area of Denver, sealed up tight with bars on windows, cars turned up into fighting positions. A Humvee sat burnt and twisted, what remained of its internals were melted with thermite grenades, as is the procedure for lost equipment, lest it fall into the hands of the enemy.

A battle had raged here, men had died as, coagulated blood marked corners used as cover. Whatever building the civilians had used was now lost, likely the apartment complex 200 meters away, as it had burned down to the blackened matchsticks of a frame. In the quiet before the storm, Evan knew they were close. Corporal Mendoza walked point along the desolate roadway, as the air shifted. "Mendoza!" Evan whispered. "Get down."

The Corporal stopped in his tracks and looked back, "What?"

Evan crept up towards the front, his head low. He peeked out just past the edge of the corner building, into the intersection.

"What do you see?" Mendoza whispered.

Evan sprinted towards the corner building. Something seemed out of place. The liquor store had thick concrete walls painted white, tall barred windows, but it wasn't an ideal spot for an ambush or defense. He pulled the phone from his pocket and set it along the building so only the camera was sticking out. His radio was going crazy, as no doubt they'd want to know what the hell was happening. He turned the volume down. "Why here?" he wondered out loud. He snapped a couple photos and zoomed in close; there was a slight bubble along the straight edge of the roof. The large red and yellow signs read 'Liquor,' 'Lotto,' 'Grocery,' and it dawned on him. "The food," he whispered.

Finally, he listened to his radio. Lieutenant Chilcot had moved past frustration into mechanical acceptance. "Do you hear me Atlas 1-1," his voice drawled. "Pick up your radio, I know you can hear me."

Evan keyed his microphone. "Sorry, Sir."

"No, you're not," Chilcot said. "What's going on?"

"You got any smoke 1-6?" Evan asked. "Got a linear danger area up here."

"Enemy contact?"

Evan hesitated. "Just come up here, Sir."

Chilcot sprinted up the right side of the road. Apartment buildings and high rises towering over them, they could be anywhere. He spotted Chilcot, hunkered down at the corner, the building used as cover.

"You really want to kill these people, Sir?"

"Where?" Chilcot panted, breathless from the run.

Evan showed him the pictures on his phone, the small outline of a marksman's head on top of the building. Quickly Chilcot bobbed his head out from beside the building, then back in.

"Atlas 1-6 and Atlas 1-1, this is Atlas 6," Captain Haegen's voice hissed through the radio.

"What's going on up there? Why has the column stopped?"

"This fucking guy…" Chilcot shook his head and picked up the hand mic. "Linear danger area, Sir. Negative contact. We'll bypass with smoke." Chilcot waited for the smoke to billow across the entire intersection.

A short time passed, a hollow hum like a bumblebee echoed off in the distance. "Atlas 16," Haegen said finally. "Incoming artillery, shot! Get your head down!"

Both Chilcot and Evan looked cockeyed at one another, as rounds slammed into the building, chunks of concrete sprayed into the street. Evan peered around the corner of the building. Bodies lay strewn across the road; some men, though mostly women, children, no older than those overseas, dead on the pavement.

"1-6, Next time you feel like bypassing a threat," Haegen growled across the radio. "You're welcome to join them."

Evan gritted his teeth, a rage building inside. He looked back, trying to spot Captain Haegen, then rose walking back towards the rear.

"What're you doing?" Chilcot yelled, running back towards him.

In silence, Evan flipped the safety off and raised his rifle.

Chilcot's hand grabbed onto his shoulder. "Don't," he whispered.

"We should have done this from the start," Evan whispered back, ripping the Lieutenant's grasp away.

"Stop," Chilcot yelled, as a large body ran up at full steam from the rear. As though he had sensed the commotion, Sergeant First Class Stokes sprinted, then lowered his shoulder, leveling Evan, knocking him to his back. Together they grabbed Evan, and dragged him around the corner and towards the smoldering ruins.

"Holy sweet Jesus," Stokes mumbled at the carnage. He walked up towards a little girl, or what was left of her, her black skin seared with fire; he knelt down beside of her. Tears filled his eyes, as surely, he was thinking of his own daughter. He looked back at Chilcot. "We've got to end this."

"Not yet." Chilcot shook his head. "Bide your time... We'll figure this out."

"Figure this out?" Stokes strained at the thought. "These aren't insurgents, Sir. What's there to figure out?"

"We're not out here alone," Chilcot said. "Whatever this is, it's bigger than us. You want a bullet in your head? Killing Haegen won't do a damn thing if we don't survive."

The anger in Stokes was palpable now, seething as he too was ready to kill. Whatever fight had been in

Evan, was gone now, and the Lieutenant's words seemed to make sense.

"Just give me a day?" Chilcot pleaded. "Figure a way out of this."

"Roger, Sir." Evan looked over at Stokes, his face snarled at the decision.

Chilcot prodded him again. "Sergeant Stokes?"

Stokes shook his head. "Whatever, Sir."

"Uhhhh." A voice grumbled in the distance.

Evan called out, "Casualty!" He ran towards the sound. The man's body was charred, his legs pinned under a slab of concrete. He recognized the man, his old camo hat flipped backwards.

"You," the man strained, staring dead at Evan, as though he recognized him too. "They're killing us," he whispered, he breath fleeting. "We tried to surrender; they wouldn't let us." His face contorted, as if something inside had just changed; the pattern of breathing shifted, fast and shallow now, his eyes frantic. "Find Nunez... fight them."

Evan's head cocked, as he remembered the photo from the briefing – Nunez' face, his eyes set low. "The drug dealer?" he mumbled, but the man didn't answer, his eyes blank and dead. Staring at the lifeless flesh, Evan felt like he could see a glimpse of his bleak future.

CHAPTER 8

Fighting intensified as they closed in on the five points, then ceased abruptly, and once more dusk fell on the battlefield. The platoons had split up along adjacent street corners, as battalion worried that enemy forces might flee the target area. Evan lay in the prone, beside a broken chunk of reinforced concrete. It was as if the enemy were ghosts and contact had simply stopped and moved towards the south without contact. *Odd*, he thought, that they would leave this avenue of approach uncovered.

Evan's mind wandered to Captain Arden... Lindsey. *Smartass little ginger. Clever too.* He smiled at the thought, and for the first time he hoped he would survive this. He was glad she wasn't out here; glad she didn't have to make these sorts of decisions. His eyes moved in and out with the shadows drifting along pavement, yet kept shifting towards a fire hydrant fifty meters ahead; something was off, a diagonal line where there shouldn't have been one. *A crack in the pavement*, he noticed, then finally set his binoculars on it. The cords were grey leading up into the base of the hydrant. On further inspection, he could see there were no bolts holding it down, and the front cap hung loose from its threading. "Atlas 1-6," he transmitted. "I need to see you at my location."

"Net call, net call, net call," Haegen's voice sounded off over the radio in darkness. "This is Atlas 6. Be advised, Bravo Company to our south is sustaining heavy fire. Be prepared to initiate a *movement to contact* in five minutes."

"Atlas 6, this is Atlas 16," Chilcot said over the radio. Evan's face flushed, his heart pounding out of his chest. If they failed here, surely, he would be shot for treason. "Recommend moving out forward of my position. We have a clear shot to outflank the enemy, and take the objective."

"1-6... good action." Haegen's words uttered with genuine exuberance. "All units, fall in on first platoon."

"First platoon," First Sergeant Baker yelled; the lead element lined up in two columns along either sidewalk. "Move out!"

They crossed the line of departure at 34th street. Second platoon moved out next, then finally the headquarters platoon in the middle. Chilcot spun quickly, staring back through his night vision goggles into a sea of green. A smaller third column had formed in the center of the street – First Lieutenant Jackson, Captain Haegen, then First Sergeant Baker, all appropriate spaced. Chilcot pumped his fist silently to himself, anticipating the kill.

"Tell me when," Evan whispered, prompting Chilcot to spin once more.

"Not yet." He moved out into the middle of the street and saw that Captain Haegen had stopped short and was offset from the hydrant, staring.

"Atlas 1-6," Haegen growled over the radio. "Care to explain the IED stuffed inside the fire hydrant?"

"Shit," Chilcot whispered, and turned to Evan. "Now!"

Evan dropped to one knee, and cut the detonation cord.

Both Chilcot and Stokes started for the rear; Sergeant Beaudry turned and followed, as Evan struck a match igniting the detonation cord in a blaze, at the end of which shot out like a claymore, spraying hundreds of pellets out like a giant sawed-off shotgun blast.

A man sprinted out of the dust up towards the head of the column, a night vision silhouette altogether different from the rest of the force, no helmet, a shorter rifle. "Quinn!" Evan raised his rifle. "Stop right there!"

"Go!" Quinn yelled, his arms and legs pumping like an Olympic sprinter. "Now's our chance!"

Towards the rear of the platoon, intermittent bursts of rifle fire rang out as both Chilcot and Stokes zeroed in on Captain Haegen, ready to finish the job.

"First Platoon!" Evan yelled. "Follow me, and haul ass!" He sprinted ahead on their route of march.

A loud metallic 'clack, clack, clack' sounded, a familiar report, like a Russian machine gun wielded by Afghani troops. Tracer rounds fired overhead, and Evan raised his hands. "CEASE FIRE!" He yelled at the top of his lungs. "Cease fire!" Finally, the shooting stopped.

"Put 'em down!" A young black man, no more than 15 years old, stepped out from the window of a red brick building, wearing a red checkered shirt and black jeans, and carrying an ancient looking Kalashnikov machine gun.

"We're not surrendering," Evan yelled. "We want to join you!"

"Uhhh…" The young man cocked his head, unsure as to what to do.

"What the hell are you doing?" Quinn whispered.

"Follow my lead," he whispered back to Quinn. "You've got an infantry company coming right behind us." Evan walked forward slowly, as he spoke. "We need to see Nunez… so, hurry the hell up."

The young man ran back towards his window and pulled out a black bar with a ninety-degree hook on the end. "C'mon." He motioned with his hand out towards the street. There he stuck the black bar inside the manhole cover and lifted. "Down here."

The sewer wasn't half as bad as Evan expected, likely since potable water had ceased to flow, so too did the toilets. No worse than a Middle Eastern bathroom, which wasn't saying much.

The young man, as Evan discovered, was somewhat of a Sergeant, or a 'Young-B,' (whatever the hell that meant) of the *Bloods* gang. "You don't talk much," Evan whispered, crouching down under a pipe. "Do you?"

Evan wondered at why the Young-B didn't try disarming the platoon, and why he was so willing to go along. Fear, maybe trust, or intelligence, or maybe he didn't care whether he lived or died.

"Na." Young-B stopped cold and lifted the left side of his shirt, exposing raised scars from old bullet wounds. "Figured it's best, keep my mouth shut." Though when he did speak, the manner in which he spoke, his tone, carried weight.

Evan respected that quality, and as he learned the military incursion into the city had done something that years of gang intervention had failed: uniting the gangs and the community under a single cause. Bloods and Cryps, MS-13, the Outlaw biker gang, smaller local gangs of every flavor, everyone with the will and means to fight.

A mile into the sewer, they reached a hub - five tunnels branching off, and what seemed like a platoon's worth of armed civilians moving from south to north across the hub. "This way," the Young-B said, motioning towards the western tunnel.

Two guards stood on either side of a ladder; one was Hispanic, the same buzzed head and tattoos Evan had seen on Nunez. The other was a formidable looking leather-clad biker, long hair and a long beard, his colors fully patched out, no doubt from his many accomplishments. Both carried pump action shotguns, the perfect weapon for close quarters.

"These guys need to see the boss," Young-B said, pointing back at the platoon.

The biker looked Evan up and down like a piece of meat. "You the leader, Staff Sergeant?"

Evan noticed the hint of an eagle, globe and anchor peeking out from below the biker's shirt sleeve, and nodded.

"No guns." The biker grabbed the hand guard of Evan's rifle, and Evan tensed, but refrained from moving. He didn't want or need to start a firefight down here. Gently, the biker unclipped the sling, and handed the rifle off to Private Hayes, then the shotgun.

Quinn handed over his rifle and pistol, grip first. "I'm going up, too."

Above the manhole was a hastily constructed plywood room, attached to the back door of a dive bar. The windows in the front were boarded up, the room lit by lanterns. A map was spread out over the pool table, green army men and matchbox cars placed strategically to track progress of the battle. The mirror behind the bar had been shattered. On closer inspection the whole room looked to be in shambles, with beer bottles broken on the floor, empty liquor bottles littered across the bar top. A single arm holding a pistol, heavily tattooed below the rolled sleeve of a dress shirt, jutted from the tall back chair placed peculiarly in the corner.

Evan reached into his pocket and grabbed a rolled-up ball of detonation cord, primed into a wad of C4. The ball uncoiled like a yoyo and came to rest nearly soundless underneath the chair. Nunez looked down. "Hah," he let out a hearty laugh. "I'm already impressed."

Evan set himself down on the edge of the pool table, his lighter poised dangerously close to the detonating cord. "Thought you'd sound a little more..."

"Mexican?" He spun the chair around.

Evan shrugged.

"I'm from L.A. there, chief..." Nunez spoke with hint of a Chicano accent he had clearly been working to get rid of. "Got myself a degree in business and everything."

"Damn." Evan smirked. "Sort of hoped you'd call me 'Esse.'"

"What's with the Delivery boy?" Nunez pointed a finger at Quinn.

Evan cocked an eyebrow. "Delivery boy?"

"Never there when you need them," Nunez winked at Quinn. "Always there when you don't."

Evan looked back at Quinn. "What's he talking about?"

"Nothing," Quinn said. "Don't listen to him."

Nunez stared dead at Quinn. "Suppose your boss just dropped off that briefcase full of cash just for the hell of it?"

Evan stared into Nunez' eyes, not a hint of a lie in them. "And?"

Nunez's eyes shifted up at the ceiling, as though harboring deep regret. "And guns… crates and crates of guns. All on one condition."

Evan could guess as he stared back at Quinn, but he chose to remain silent.

"Go to war with the police, he said." Nunez slammed his pistol down on the arm of the chair. "Didn't know they'd come back at us with the whole fuckin' Army!"

"Liar," Quinn growled.

"You don't know!" Nunez aimed his pistol at Quinn, his off-hand feeling along his pants pocket. "But I've got proof."

"Almost got me." Evan shook his head. "Just for a second, I thought a drug lord could ever be the victim, as if you hadn't killed, hadn't polluted the minds of- "

"Hey!" Nunez cut him off. "Never said I was a saint, far from it. I can still care about this neighborhood, these people. And don't tell me you never killed, Soldier boy." He pointed once more, this time with his pistol. "I can see it in your eyes." He settled back in the chair; his pistol still aimed at Evan. "People want what I've got. So, what, if they want to kill themselves snorting that shit? Far be it from me to tell them how to live their lives."

Evan shook his head. "Bullshit."

"Oh?" Nunez stared at Evan knowingly. "What's that bottle of pills rattling around in your pocket? Bet it ain't vitamins."

"This?" Evan pulled the bottle of painkillers from his pocket and rattled the contents around. "You might as well be handing out death certificates."

Nunez' eyes narrowed on him. "Which you'd willingly accept."

Evan gritted his teeth and stuffed the bottle back into his pocket. He knew Nunez was right.

"Anyway," Nunez folded his hand over his pistol in his lap. "It's too late. We're down to less than 70. By tomorrow, this whole area will be flooded with military and we will have lost."

"Then leave," Evan said.

"Where?" Nunez held his hands out. "Where would we go?"

"The whole northeastern axis is abandoned." Evan flipped his radio on. "You could use the sewers, move past any remaining forces… get out of the city."

"That's not what I meant." Nunez rested the slide of his pistol against the side of his head. "This is our home… our- "

"Roger, be advised, I have three heat signatures inside the building." The pilot's smooth voice sounded across the radio. Then another voice, "Target is marked with incendiary grenade, in 3… 2… 1… Mark."

A blast echoed just outside of the building; fragments peppered against the boarded-up windows. "Shit!" Nunez dove for cover. "That's us."

"Roger Atlas 6," the pilot said. "engaging with Vulcan." Moments later .30 caliber rounds ripped through the building.

Once the dust settled, Evan looked over and Nunez lay silent and trembling. The bullet had hit him in the right side of the lower abdomen, nearly ripping him in two. Nunez looked down, his guts spilling from his abdominal cavity. His hand shook as he reached down into his pants pocket and pulled out his car keys. 'Proof,' he mouthed, and his arm slumped lifeless to the floor.

"Good hit, Hammer 1-9," Haegen yelled over the radio. "Next run, hit it with rockets."

"Go!" Evan stuffed the keys into his pocket and ran for the manhole. He jumped and hit the sewer floor as a crash reverberated above. "Run!" Plumes of dust swirled down into the open space, then gave way to collapse. He looked back from the rear of the platoon, now heading north, what hope remained for Denver now lay in rubble at the pit of the sewer. Evan pushed against the column, afraid that the next round would be a sidewinder or JDAM, possibly an artillery barrage to bring the entire sewer system crashing down around them.

"What'd he give you?" Quinn whispered.

Evan felt inside his pocket. The keys seemed as such, just keys. Then he felt it – the plastic shroud of a thumb drive. "Just keys." Quickly, he spun it against the key ring, cracking the thumb drive eyelet apart and lifted only the keys from his pocket. "Maybe he wanted us to take his car."

Quinn strained, confounded as he ran his fingers over the BMW keys.

114 Tread: Fallen Nation

CHAPTER 9

Miles away, near the edge of Denver proper, the sewer system was no longer large enough for a platoon to reasonably move through. Hayes was the first one out, then Evan, then Quinn, then the whole of what remained of the platoon.

"Hey, Atlas 1-1… Sergeant Decker," a familiar voice sounded over the radio. "This is your commander."

"Don't answer," Quinn whispered.

"I know you're out there," Haegen hissed. "I know you took my Soldiers. I want them back… If you give them back, I might let you live. Hell, I may even still bring you into the fold."

Evan picked up the hand mic, ready to respond.

Quinn shook his head. "Don't do it."

"I want you to know that I killed Lieutenant Chilcot and Sergeant First Class Stokes… I will admit that I had a little help. And I know you're the one that set that IED. That makes it personal. That hurt a little bit, deep down." Evan could sense the sick bastard smiling on the other side of the radio. "Once we're in control of the country, I promise I will find you, and I will take everything from you, I will destroy everything and everyone you love… and once you're completely broken, I'll kill you too. That is, unless you come back."

"Atlas 6, this is Atlas 1-1." Evan glared in a vicious sneer. "Fuck off, Sir."

"I knew you were there 1-1." Evan could sense the grin widen in Captain Haegen's voice. "There's one other thing… Your little crush Captain Arden, my ex-wife, Daisy Duke, whatever the hell you call her… I'm gonna do terrible things to her, too."

"You won't fucking touch her," Evan whispered. His mind frantic, he pulled the notebook from his shoulder pocket and flipped through page after page looking for the battalion command frequency.

"Struck a nerve, did I?" Captain Haegen chuckled as he continued to taunt her. "Give me what I want and I'll leave her- "

"Break, break, break!" The radio squelched with a high-pitched screech. "Atlas 6, this is Wolf 9… Did I just hear you threaten me?"

"Stay out of this, Lindsey," Haegen growled over the radio. No question now that he was frustrated with the turn. "This is bigger than me or you, and I'll do what I need to, even if that means sacrificing *you*."

"You're insane, Jim!" Captain Arden yelled out over the radio. Evan figured that she would have been towards the south of the city still, back in the staging area. At least a half hour by car, only minutes by helicopter.

"Sergeant Decker," her voice calmed. "Go to the place we talked about."

"What? No!" Evan yelled. "I'm coming to get you."

"Go to the place, Evan. I'll be fine." Her voice strained, as though something was happening on her end. "The place with the boulder."

"Captain Arden?" He waited. "Lindsey… are you there?"

A new voice sounded. "Atlas 1-1, this is Wolf 6. It's Colonel Trajan, son. I need you to come back in before things get more out of hand than they already are."

"I saw you there, Sir," Evan spoke, frantically. "I was outside the room when he choked the life out of Captain Sayyid. I know this isn't you, it isn't what you want."

Colonel Trajan keyed the hand mic and let out a long sigh. "It's not what any of us want, but it's here nonetheless."

"Then fight, Sir. Stand up against this."

"You won't win this, son. They're too powerful, too deeply embedded. Now, you have a choice. Either sit here on the radio while we triangulate your position and Captain Haegen moves on you, or you can go… take your chances that we won't come after you."

"And Captain Arden?"

"I promise," Colonel Trajan said. "I won't let him touch a hair on her head."

"Wolf 6, this is Atlas 6," Captain Haegen interrupted. "You'd be wise to remember your station, Sir."

"And you'd be wise to remember yours, Captain," Colonel Trajan roared. "For the time being, I'm still in charge of you."

Evan's stomach felt sick to the point of vomiting. It was a feeling of loss he had never felt; the painkillers couldn't dull this pain, couldn't take it away, and what's more, he was powerless once again. With that, he turned the radio off and moved his way to the lead of the column.

Within eyeshot northwest of their position was a large modern building, a white stone veneer and brushed metal, jutting off at odd angles; large windows that spanned the entire three stories up. Outside was a large red and black sign, a name he had never heard, yet clearly important enough to have a high school named after him. His thoughts turned desperate as they turned the corner to the rear of the school, a bus parking lot.

"Hayes," Evan whispered. "Go hotwire me one of those busses."

Hayes looked at him cockeyed, as though he'd gone insane.

"I know, I know. You're black, and I'm being racist" Evan quipped. "You gonna hotwire me a bus or what?"

A sour look grew on Hayes' face. "Man, that's racist, what the- "

"I got it," Young-B said, walking his way up from the pack and onto the nearest bus.

"See," Evan said. "Nothing personal, I just need someone to hotwire the fucking bus." The bus engine strained and Evan hustled the group on.

"What now?" Staff Sergeant Cass asked.

"You go," Evan said. "Lead them. Get the hell out of here."

Cass thought for a moment. "You're not coming with us."

"I'll catch up." Evan stepped off of the bus stairwell. "Maybe."

"But you don't even know where we're going!" Cass yelled from the open doorway.

"I know! That way I won't give you guys up!" He darted towards the front of the building, where several cars were left abandoned.

Cass nodded, in a moment of final clarity. The bus started to roll, then suddenly screeched to a halt and two people stepped out and ran in Evan's direction.

"You guys lost or something?" Evan yelled, looking around for any movement apart from them, as he located a sedan and smashed the driver's side window out.

"Or something." Quinn said, his pace slowing to a walk.

"No, seriously," Evan said, sitting down on the broken glass, and leaning under the steering column. "What're you doing?"

"You're gonna need help," Hayes said. "And I'm not hanging out with Staff Sergeant Cass. He's a bigger dick than you, and dumber than a bag of rocks."

Evan shrugged. "Your funeral." He turned to Quinn. "And what's your stake?"

"You let me worry about that."

"What the hell?" Hayes asked, as the engine of the sedan fired up. "You know how to hotwire a car?"

"I'm a farm boy, Hayes. I can do damn near anything." Evan smirked. "One of these days I'm gonna teach you about delegating authority."

'Snip,' Evan cut through the first barrier of concertina wire, a jagged spool with razor spikes on the ends. Hayes pulled back the length and the trio walked inside.

"Act natural," Quinn said, slowing to a walk. The morning light had just started to crest over the horizon of FOB Bronco.

Hayes cocked his head. "We about to get caught and you wanna *act natural."*

"Pretend we're roving patrol," Evan whispered.

Hayes pointed at Quinn. "This guy's not even wearing the same uniform. You think they'll think we're on patrol?"

"Shut up," Quinn whispered, watching a pair of Soldiers approach. "Mornin' fellas!"

The Soldiers nodded and went on their way.

Quinn cocked his head back and smirked. "See? I've been in law enforcement a long time… best way to keep from getting caught is just pretend you didn't do a damn thing."

Evan's brow furrowed, thinking of the thumb drive in his pocket.

"Command tent's over here," Quinn whispered.

"Stop." Evan grabbed the back of Quinn's shirt. "You stay outside, I'll go."

Quinn's eyes narrowed. "Listen- "

"No," Evan growled. "You listen. I don't know what your game is. We're on good terms for the moment, but don't mistake that for trust. Stand guard." He didn't wait for a reply, quickly turning and entering the command tent.

A sliver of light shone on Colonel Trajan, asleep on his cot. His hand lay poised on the grip of his Sig Sauer pistol resting on his chest. Evan waved his hand across his face, just to check, then slowly, delicately moved his hand onto the slide.

Trajan's finger twitched and in an instant Evan snatched the pistol and turned it on Trajan's head.

"What… the fuck… are you doing, Sergeant?" Trajan whispered.

"Where's Captain Arden?"

Trajan glared as though through sight alone, he could strike Evan dead. "Give my fucking pistol back and we can talk."

Evan hesitated.

In less than a moment, Trajan swung, grabbing the pistol, ripping it from Evan's grasp.

Evan jumped back and raised his rifle.

Trajan confidently holstered his weapon. "You damn well don't take a commander's pistol, unless you plan on using it."

Evan cocked his head, confused at the turn. "Where is she?"

"Captain Arden?" Trajan asked, bending down to pick up his camouflage blouse. "Officially, she's escaped. Unofficially, I sent her away with a team. I'm getting as many of us out as I can."

"Why?" Evan asked, though he wasn't sure what he was asking *why* to.

"It's not safe," he said, zipping up his top. "Not for you or me, or anyone else."

"You're staying, Sir?"

"Someone's got to try," Trajan said. "I'll be that asshole. As for you, get the hell out of here. I know where you're going, and if I make it out of this alive, I may call on you."

Evan nodded. He didn't fully understand to what depth the conspiracy went, but he was confident that Colonel Trajan would be one of a few he trusted to fight it, even if he had let Captain Sayyid die.

As Evan turned to leave, Colonel Trajan grabbed his arm. "Six months ago, you received what you thought was a flu shot. As did a select majority of the country… It wasn't for the flu."

Evan cocked an eyebrow. "The virus?"

Trajan nodded. "Find the vaccine… for those you love."

Evan nodded his head. "Roger, Sir." Though, the prospect of doing so seemed irrelevant at the moment.

"Where's Quinn?" Evan pulled the flap of the tent shut.

Hayes shook his head and pointed.

"Motherfucker," Evan growled.

They 'acted natural,' while walking back to the breech, as Quinn suggested. Up ahead a group of Soldiers gathered, talking amongst themselves while examining the break in the concertina wire. Abruptly Hayes spun.

"What the hell are you doing?" Evan whispered, slowly turning his course away from the group of Soldiers.

"Fuck this," Hayes whispered back. "I'm outa here."

"Hey you!" The voice sounded like Major Phillips. "Get back here."

Evan's pace quickened, as Hayes broke out in a sprint. "Damnit," Evan mumbled, then broke out in a sprint after him.

There was a rumble in the distance, and quickly approaching headlights. An up-armor Humvee swung to a stop in front of Hayes, whose rifle was trained on the vehicle.

The driver's side windows opened. "Get in!" Quinn yelled.

Both Hayes and Evan piled into the back, as bullets began to ricochet off the armor plating. "Go!" Evan shouted, as Quinn jammed on the accelerator. He swung the vehicle around and aimed for the group of Soldiers gathered at the wire.

"What the hell are you doing?" Evan yelled. "You'll kill them."

Quinn gritted his teeth. "They'll move."

Evan reached up from behind and grabbed the steering wheel, trying to pull him off course. Quinn whipped his elbow back, striking Evan in the jaw.

Quinn hammered down on the accelerator, ready to run over anything in his path. A single Soldier stayed in place, and ricocheted off the Humvee's passenger side bumper.

Evan opened the rear window, and stuck his head out, thankful that the Soldier was still moving. He turned to Quinn. "What the hell are you thinking?"

Quinn glared back. "I think a *thank you* is in order."

"You almost got us killed, almost ran that guy over."

Quinn rolled his eyes and shook his head.

"Where were you?" Evan asked.

"Taking care of some things." Quinn took a hard, black case off the passenger seat and set it on the floor. "And getting the Humvee… You're welcome, by the way."

"Whatever," Evan said sarcastically, eyeing the case. "Where we headed?"

"Away from the city for now." Quinn turned off onto a dirt road. "We'll head north… Wyoming. That's where you're from, isn't it?"

How does he know that? Evan wondered. "Sure."

"What'd Trajan tell you?" Quinn's voice seemed too nonchalant to be asking in passing. "Where's your lady-friend headed?"

"Nothing." Evan wondered why he felt so compelled to lie right now. "Just told me to go."

"And Captain Arden?" Quinn pressed. "He didn't say anything?"

"He said she made it out, that was all."

"Hmmm." Quinn glanced back at Evan. "She'll be headed north, too. We'll try to catch up to her."

"Cut the crap, Quinn." Evan leaned up between the seats. "What's your interest in her?"

Quinn shook his head. "Nothing, man. Just trying to help a brother out."

"Bullshit," Evan mumbled, looking out east towards a rising sun. They drove north, through plains and grasslands, along rural roads parallel with interstate 25.

By mid-day, they passed Cheyanne. Fifty miles north, Evan woke to the sound of a sputtering engine.

"Relax," Quinn said. "There's a spare gas can mounted on the back." He pulled off the side of the road.

Evan wondered why they hadn't seen Captain Arden. Maybe she hadn't taken backroads. Maybe she hadn't made it at all. He stepped out of the Humvee to stretch.

A steady stream of expletives issued from the rear of the Humvee, and Evan walked back towards Quinn.

"Empty." Evan smirked. "Isn't it?"

Quinn gritted his teeth, and punched the empty can.

"Bad spot to be out of gas," Evan said. "Not another town for at least 10 miles."

Quinn walked off down the road, then *screamed* in a guttural roar. Evan noticed the limp, the slight shine of blood coming off of Quinn's cargo pants.

Evan cracked open the door, Hayes lounging in the back seat. "Grab your gear," Evan said. "We're walking."

"What the hell?" Hayes threw his assault pack out onto the pavement.

"Out of gas," Evan said. "Another ten miles up the road, town of Wheatland. We can steal a few cars, go our separate ways."

Hayes cocked his head. "Thought we were sticking together."

Evan shook his head. "You don't want to go where I'm going."

"Hayes grabbed is rifle and stepped out of the Humvee. "Couldn't be *that* bad."

"Last time I left was on pretty bad terms. I don't want you guys all wrapped up in my bull- "

"He's right." Quinn huffed, shaking off frustration. "We're fugitives now, and safer together."

"You're not hearing me," Evan growled. "Neither of you are coming with me." He looked down at Quinn's leg. "I'll patch you up, but that's it."

CHAPTER 10

Wind blew colder now under a grey sky, each frigid step north a torment. "How much farther, Sergeant?" Hayes stared up the embankment, one of a dozen they would have to cross. The sun shone, but just barely through the hazy sky.

"Don't call me that," Evan snapped. "Few hours maybe."

Hayes reached into his pocket, counting out cigarettes. "What'll I call you then?"

"Nothing." Evan's pace quickened.

Hayes stuffed the cigarettes back in his pocket, jogged along to catch up. "I'll have to call you something, If not Sergeant."

"Why are you here?" The impulse of annoyance had long since past; growing into a rage. "Why are you following me? Don't you have somewhere to go?"

"I trust you…" Hayes coughed, winded at the pace. "Kept me safe for so long. Like family."

Evan shook his head. "Not like family."

"I wouldn't know… I don't have one. Grew up in Detroit, foster care system."

Evan stopped dead in his tracks, staring down Hayes; impulsive, immature, undisciplined. "My responsibility," he muttered.

"What's now?"

"Evan." He gritted his teeth. "Call me Evan." He started back along the road. "Don't expect to be welcomed with open arms."

Hayes laughed. "Town's a little vanilla then?"

Evan shook his head. "The last time I was there… let's just say people died."

Hayes' looked back. "And what about Agent Quinn?"

"Forget him," Evan mumbled, looking back at Quinn, some 200 meters back. "He won't keep up… and I don't trust him."

The road was blocked into Wheatland. Armed men stood guard at a barricade of pickup trucks. Both Evan and Hayes were tired, hungry, and in no place to refuse a meal.

"Stay back!" one of the men shouted. He was stocky, wearing a red flannel shirt and bushy beard. "Sickness has killed over half of us, you can turn right around."

"We don't want any trouble," Evan yelled back. "I'm going to Cowley." He took a single step forward.

The man gripped his rifle tighter. "You can take the trail." He pointed off west with his barrel. "Goes up through the mountains, out of town."

"You get a flu shot?" Evan inched forward; his voice as soothing as possible. "Maybe six months ago?"

"Yea…" The man cocked his head. "Why?"

"That saved your life, boss." Evan inched forward once more. "So long as someone hasn't been living under a rock, the dead are dead, the living are immune."

"Stay back." The man aimed at Evan. "How do you know that?"

"A little birdie told me." Evan looked back. Quinn was just walking up to their position. "No kidding, a colonel, name of Trajan." Evan inched forward again.

"Stay back, I said!"

"Enough!" Quinn shouted. "We are not going to get you sick. I can vouch for his story." He pulled his wallet out and produced a federal badge. "Have you seen a woman come through here? Dressed like these guys."

The man's shoulders relaxed, though the rifle remained trained on Evan. "Haven't seen anyone for days."

"That's fine." Quinn stepped forward, right up to the rifle. "We'd like to spend the night, maybe get some hot chow if you'd let us."

The man's eyes narrowed on Quinn. "What've you got to trade?"

Quinn looked back down the road. "There's a Humvee about ten miles from here. Give it some gas and it's all yours." He leaned in to whisper in the man's ear, inaudible to Evan, until he said, "And if she does show up, let her know that he's here."

The man looked over at his buddies for approval, then nodded. "Alright."

Evan looked strangely at Quinn.

"What?" Quinn said. "Can't I help a guy out?"

The stout man's name was Duncan, or Dunc for short; the town of Wheatland was a small farming community along interstate 25. They had embraced the idea of community, as they had since their inception. In a town like that, everyone knows everyone – their strengths and weaknesses, accomplishments and failings. For that very reason, Evan feared going home.

The meal was served in a large barn setting. It reminded Evan of the American equivalent to a Viking *Great Hall*. Long tables were set up down the length of the barn. Families sat in congress with one another, talking, embracing. Evan missed that feeling of community, even if he could never have it again.

Dunc found them an open area to sit, served up plates of hot corn and oatmeal, a small portion of beef. Then he walked over to a tall curly haired man seated at the head table. He knelt down and whispered into his ear for a long while. Evan watched as the man's facial expressions changed with each new bit of information.

Once the barn was near full, and everyone was served, the tall man stood.

"Welcome to our new guests!" He turned to them. "I'm Mayor Brown."

The room gasped. For all they knew, the virus was still an active threat.

"Calm down, everyone," Mayor Brown said. "According to our new guests, the sickness is no longer a threat, as I'm sure they'll explain. And I'm sure they'll explain what all they're doing here, and what's going on in the outside world." There was a certain demand to his voice. "Won't you, fellas?"

"Sure." Evan rose, chewing a mouthful of corn. "I don't know how- "

Quinn grabbed him. "Sit down, junior." He stood and faced the tall man. "Our nation has fallen. When I came to learn the truth of the matter, it was too late. They disabled the communications network to destroy any chance of a response. They inoculated certain individuals... those they deemed 'useful.' All others were left to die. They'll start with the cities, clear them out, relocate individuals to work camps, mines and manufacturing- "

"Who's they?" Mayor Brown interrupted, quelling a surge in the crowd, though the whispers persisted.

"Us," Quinn said. "Our government, our elites here and abroad, their operatives within the bureaucracy and major corporations."

Odd, Evan thought, that Mayor Brown didn't so much as flinch at the bombshell information. "Quinn," Evan whispered.

Quinn's nostrils flared, upset at the interruption. "They will break our population, turn us into slaves…"

The room erupted in nervous chatter.

"Quiet, everyone!" Mayor Brown yelled. "What proof do you have of this?"

"What proof do you need?" Quinn asked. "It's happening as we speak."

Mayor Brown sat back down, his hand rubbing anxiously at his chin.

"When they come, and they will," Evan stood back up, shoving Quinn to the side. "You need to be ready to fight."

Mayor brown threw his hands up. "What good will it do?"

"I don't know…" Evan shook his head. "I'd rather die free than live as a slave."

Mayor Brown didn't speak for the rest of the night, nor did Evan and his group. What was said cast a foreboding dread over the room. The joy the town had felt simply in one another's company would end.

After dinner, Dunc escorted them to his farm. "You can sleep in here," he said, opening his barn door.

"I've slept in worse places," Evan mumbled.

Dunc handed each of them a scratchy woolen blanket, then said, "I'm collecting rainwater in the barrels. Feel free to top up."

As Dunc left for his house, Quinn looked for a suitably soft and dry bed, and found it on a set of hay bales.

Evan waited till the door was closed, then stood over Quinn. "What'd you have to do that for?"

"What's that?" Quinn shifted his hands behind his head. "Tell them the truth?"

"Take away their hope."

Quinn closed his eyes. "If you knew there was a fight coming, wouldn't you want to know?"

Evan suppressed the urge to kick Quinn squarely in the ribs. "You make it seem like we're all doomed."

"That's because we are."

"*No*." Evan nearly spit the word. "I don't think so."

Quinn opened a single eye, peering up at Evan. "Best you can hope is to run long enough that they stop chasing."

"Bullshit," Evan said. "I'm not running."

"We're here, because you decided to run."

Evan huffed, kicked at the dirt. Quinn had a point, but still, if there was any way Evan could fight back, he would. Maybe just not here and not now. As always, he took a pill and tried to relax. Perhaps he was doomed and just didn't accept it yet.

CHAPTER 11

Zero dark thirty, Evan felt a drip of water land on his forehead, then trickle into his eye. It didn't sting, yet it reminded him of his last roadside bomb. Either way, he didn't dare move. Something was happening in the blackness, yet he couldn't tell what. A noise came from where Quinn was sleeping. A crack of moonlight, Evan looked over and Hayes lay asleep a few feet away. *What's Quinn up to?* Evan wondered.

There were whispers outside, quiet, as two ships passing in the night. The door cracked again, a silhouette, then black. Quiet footsteps, quieter than Quinn and without a limp, coming directly toward Evan. He didn't dare move. Only his hand shifted, already gripping the rifle, he flipped off the safety.

He could sense her now as she touched his hand in the darkness. In an instant, his trigger finger relaxed. His body still paralyzed, all he could mutter was, "Lindsey?"

Her forehead pressed to his, her gentle touch grazing his cheek, as two long lost friends and lovers. "I'm here," she whispered, softly pressing her lips to his.

He shuddered, his heart beating out of his chest, as her hand wrapped under his head, drawing him in close to her. "We need to go," she whispered. "Specialist Sinclair is not who he says he is."

"What?" He shot up. His flashlight shone over by Quinn's bed. "Where is he?"

"I passed him on the way in," Lindsey said. "Using the bathroom. I told him to be careful."

'Pop, pop.' The echo of a rifle issued.

"Hayes!" Evan shook the private awake. "We gotta go."

"What's that?" Hayes shook the sleep from his face. "Who's shooting?"

Evan looked back at Lindsey.

"One of my guys," she whispered, drawing her pistol from its holster. "Be careful."

Evan dropped the night vision over his eyes and the world became a sea of green. Hayes stacked behind him on the door, as they had done so many times. Evan whispered, "3, 2, 1," and 'crack,' he put his shoulder into the door and hustled down the outer wall of the barn.

They stacked again at the corner of the building. Evan peered around the side. Two bodies lay dead on the ground, two more standing. Evan could see the shimmer of glass from another pair of night vision goggles, Sinclair held a pistol to Quinn's head.

"Let him go!" Evan yelled.

"Quinn's the enemy!" Sinclair yelled back. Evan expected a carbon copy of Captain Haegen, but this Sinclair's tone was disturbed. "Do you know how many of us have died because of him? And for what…?"

"Take the shot," Quinn said, gripping Sinclair's arm wrapped around his neck.

"For what?" Evan asked. Deep down, he could feel something unsettling about Sinclair, something that Quinn knew, or something he had done. "I want to know Quinn, what did you do, and why?"

"I didn't do a damn thing," Quinn yelled. "This motherfucker's in with Haegen, now take the damn shot!"

"What did you do?" Evan shouted.

"Tell him," the Sinclair yelled, his tone increasingly agitated. "Let him know how you sold your soul for- "

A blinding light hit them all at once. Evan and Hayes, Sinclair all tore at their faces, blinded by Captain Arden's flashlight. The round chambered with a metallic crunch. She flipped the safety off and fired.

Once Evan's eyes acclimated, he saw that Sinclair lay dead on the ground. "No!"

"What?" Lindsey screamed, shocked at his reaction. "What'd I do?"

"Tell me what you did." Evan raised his rifle and moved on Quinn. "Nunez knew something, had some dirt on you... Specialist Sinclair knew what it was. Tell me."

"Believe me when I say," Quinn dropped to his knees and put his hands behind his head. "I am on the right side of this, and this dirt you're talking about is a secret so big that I shouldn't know about it. Hell, I don't want to know about it, and I'm only doing you a favor, and keeping you safe by keeping my damn mouth shut."

"Tell me." Evan pressed the muzzle of his barrel against Quinn's temple. "Now."

"No." Quinn closed his eyes. "I'm no threat to you, but do what you have to."

"Evan," Lindsey whispered. "Put the gun down." She walked over to him slowly and put her hand on his arm.

Evan strained, gritting his teeth, squeezing the grip, and finally succumb. He felt weak. For all he knew, Quinn could be a mass murderer, or a saint. The picture hadn't grown any clearer, rather it became more convoluted than ever.

In the commotion, Dunc had woken up, and now stood before three bodies, shotgun in hand. "Probably should have said something before… I'm the sheriff of this town."

"I can explain," Evan said abruptly. "See what happened was- "

"Relax," Dunc said. "I saw just about everything. I think you all owe the lady a debt of gratitude." He looked down. "And you in particular, Mr. Quinn."

"We can fill out any written reports you need, take care of the burial." Lindsey said. "You just let us know."

"It's fine. I can handle it." Dunc shook his head. "Just, we haven't had a killing in my town since I took office... damn."

"They should all be buried with honors," Hayes said.

Everyone stared, surprised that such a consideration had come from Hayes, but people would be surprised by him in the days to come.

They didn't have a bugle, or seven riflemen in full dress with three rounds each, and there were no next of kin there to receive the flag. But they had a trumpet, and townsfolk to fire the 21-gun salute, and they had a flag, folded and displayed in the city hall. Three grave mounds were left, with hand carved tombstones.

Dunc took the liberty of hand making a wooden sign, the words, "This flag is presented on behalf of a grateful nation, as a token of appreciation, for the honorable and faithful service rendered by these Soldiers. May God bless, and keep all of the casualties of this second civil war."

The following day, their journey continued.

142 Tread: Fallen Nation

EPILOGUE

"I'm looking for a few people," Sergeant Beaudry extended his hand out. "Few of 'em dressed like me, the other, a black guy, dressed in all black fatigues. You seen 'em?"

Dunc shook the man's hand, the base of his thumb rubbed up against what seemed like an oblong bump. He looked down, a fresh wound in the shape of an eye at the crux of Beaudry's thumb and forefinger. "Haven't seen anyone for days." Dunc came off as nervous, and he knew it. "More than likely if they did pass through, they'd have taken the western trail up through the mountains."

"Mhm…" Beaudry nodded, pointing ahead towards town. "And that Humvee up the way, where'd that come from?"

"I…" Dunc stuttered, as Beaudry raised the barrel of his rifle and flipped the safety off.

"Atlas 6, this is Atlas 1-2," Beaudry said into his hand mic. "They've headed north through Wheatland, and this sheriff here is gonna tell me everything I need to know." He let go of the hand mic. "Or I'm gonna bring a whole infantry company up here to wipe you off the map… sound good?"

Dunc nodded feverishly.

"Roger, Atlas 1-2," Haegen transmitted back. "Keep me advised."

Beaudry smiled. "So, tell me where to find them."

CONNECT

For updates on upcoming projects, as well as past works, please visit the author on his website www.demarcowriter.com or on his Amazon author page.

Author Jeff DeMarco owns a writing and editing business that specializes in industrial technical writing. A former US Army Field Artillery officer and veteran, Jeff's immersion in the profession of arms and a lifelong passion for science fiction lend the characters in his richly layered post-apocalyptic military sci fi unparalleled authenticity.

A family man, Jeff hangs his hat in the thumb of Michigan, along with his wife and three kids. He enjoys writing (of course), fishing, cycling and backpacking.

Check out his apocalyptic sci fi thrillers in the *Ruler of Ashes* series or her non-profit work with the *#WolfPackAuthors Anthology*.

45689923R00081

Made in the USA
Lexington, KY
18 July 2019